DISNEP · PIXAR
COCO

randomhousekids.com

ISBN 978-0-7364-3806-3 (pbk) — ISBN 978-0-7364-3807-0 (hc)

Printed in the United States of America

10 9 8 7 6 5 4 3

Disney · PIXAR
COCO

The Junior Novelization

Adapted by Angela Cervantes

Random House New York

Prologue

Sometimes Miguel Rivera thought he was cursed. If he was, it wasn't his fault. It was because of something that happened before he was even born.

Long ago, in the town of Santa Cecilia, there was a family with a mamá, a papá, and a little girl. Their house was always full of joy—and music. The papá played guitar. The mamá and the girl danced. And everyone sang.

But the music in the happy house wasn't enough for the papá. His dream was to play for the world. So one day, he left with his guitar and never returned.

Miguel didn't know what happened after that for the musician. But he sure knew what the mamá had done. The story of Mamá Imelda had been handed down in the Rivera family for generations.

Imelda didn't waste one tear on that walk-away musician! She banished all music from her life, throwing away instruments and records, and found a job. Was it making candy? Fireworks? Sparkly underwear for wrestlers? No!

Mamá Imelda made shoes. And so did her daughter. And then her son-in-law. And her grandkids. The Rivera business and the family grew in sync. While music tore the family apart, shoes held them together.

Miguel heard this story each year on Día de los Muertos: the Day of the Dead. He used to hear it from his Mamá Coco, but she didn't remember much anymore. This year, she sat in a wicker wheelchair, vacantly staring at the ofrenda, that special place in their house where Miguel's family placed remembrances of and gifts for their ancestors to honor them.

Miguel kissed her cheek. "Hola, Mamá Coco."

"How are you, Julio?"

Miguel sighed. Sometimes Mamá Coco had trouble remembering things, like his name. But that made her the best secret-keeper! He told her pretty much everything—things he couldn't tell his abuelita, who ran their household with an iron fist.

If Abuelita said he needed to eat more tamales, then Miguel ate more tamales.

If Abuelita wanted a kiss on her cheek, then Miguel kissed her cheek.

And if Abuelita caught Miguel blowing a tune over the top of a soda bottle—"No music!"—then Miguel would stop.

Abuelita even yelled at passersby. "No music!" to the truck driver blaring his radio. "No music!" to the gentlemen singing while they strolled down the street. Her ban on music had affected all the aunts, uncles, and cousins, too.

Miguel was pretty sure they were the only family in Mexico that hated music. The worst part was that no one in his family seemed to care.

No one, that is, but him.

Chapter 1

Leaving the family home behind, Miguel breathed the crisp air of another sunny morning in Santa Cecilia. As he headed into town with his shoeshine box, he passed a woman sweeping a stoop. She waved.

"Hola, Miguel!"

"Hola." Miguel waved back. Closer to town, Miguel smiled at a lone guitar player plucking away at a song. The farther in Miguel went, the more music filled the air. Church bells chimed in harmony. A band played an upbeat tune. A radio blared a swift cumbia rhythm. Miguel soaked it all in. He couldn't help tapping out a beat on a table covered with brightly colored wooden animal figurines.

As Miguel rushed past another stand with pastries for sale, he grabbed a pan dulce and tossed the vendor a coin.

Smelling the sweet bread, Miguel's canine sidekick, Dante, sidled up to him. Miguel tore off a piece of the bread and Dante chomped it down.

Everywhere Miguel looked, people were preparing for their loved ones to return from the Land of the Dead by hanging colorful papel picado and laying marigold petals at their doorways.

As usual, Mariachi Plaza was full of musicians strolling around, waiting for their chance to serenade a couple or a family with a love song or a classic corrido. Soon a tour group gathered around a large statue of a mariachi player in the center of the plaza.

"And right here, in this very plaza, the young Ernesto de la Cruz took his first steps toward becoming the most beloved singer in Mexican history," said the guide.

Everyone in the group nodded, familiar with the legendary musician and singer. Along with the tourists, Miguel gazed up at the statue. He'd seen it a hundred times, but it always inspired him.

After a moment, Miguel found a spot in the plaza

and pulled out his shoeshine box. A mariachi plopped down for a shine.

Miguel knew the mariachi would enjoy this story. After all, everyone loved Ernesto.

"He started out a total nobody from Santa Cecilia, like me," said Miguel. "But when he played music, he made people fall in love with him. He starred in movies. He had the coolest guitar. He could fly!" Miguel had seen that special effect in some old film clips. "And he wrote the best songs! But my all-time favorite? It's——" Miguel gestured to some musicians nearby, who were playing "Remember Me," Ernesto's biggest hit. "He lived the kind of life you dream about. Until 1942, when he was crushed by a giant bell."

The mariachi looked pointedly at his shoes, which Miguel was only halfheartedly shining.

Ignoring the musician, Miguel shrugged off Ernesto's unfortunate death. "I wanna be just like him. Sometimes I look at Ernesto and I get this feeling, like we're connected somehow. Like if *he* could play music, maybe someday *I* can, too." Miguel sighed. "If it wasn't for my family."

"Ay-yi-yi, muchacho," said the mariachi, snapping Miguel out of his story.

"Huh?" said Miguel.

"I asked for a shoeshine, not your life story," replied the mariachi.

"Oh, yeah, sorry." Miguel lowered his head and polished the man's shoe. As he worked, the mariachi casually plucked at his guitar strings. "I just can't really talk about any of this at home, so—"

"Look, if I were you? I'd march right up to my family and say, 'Hey! I'm a musician. Deal with it.'"

"I could never say that."

"You ARE a musician, no?"

"I don't know. I mean, I only really play for myself—"

"Ahh!" the mariachi howled. "Did Ernesto de la Cruz become the world's best musician by hiding his sweet, sweet skills? No! He walked out onto that plaza and he played out loud!" The mariachi pointed to the gazebo, where a giant canvas that read TALENT SHOW was being unfurled. "Ah! Mira, mira! They're setting up for tonight. The music competition for Día de los Muertos. You wanna be like your hero? You should sign up!"

"Uh-uh—my family would freak," Miguel said.

"Look, if you're too scared, then, well, have fun making shoes." The mariachi shrugged. "C'mon, what did Ernesto de la Cruz always say?"

"'Seize your moment'?" Miguel said.

The mariachi looked Miguel over and then offered him his guitar. "Show me what you got, muchacho. I'll be your first audience."

Miguel's eyebrows rose. The mariachi really wanted to hear him play? He glanced down the street to make sure the coast was clear of any family members. He reached for the guitar. Once it was cradled in his arms, Miguel spread his fingers across the strings, anticipating his chord, and—

"Miguel!" a familiar voice yelled.

Miguel gasped and threw the guitar back into the mariachi's lap. Abuelita marched toward him. Tío Berto and Prima Rosa followed close behind with supplies from the market.

"Abuelita!" Miguel exclaimed.

"What are you doing here?" she asked.

"Um . . . uh . . . ," Miguel stammered as he quickly packed away his shine rag and polishes. Abuelita didn't wait for Miguel's answer. She barreled up to the mariachi and struck him with her shoe. "You leave my grandson alone!"

"Doña, please—I was just getting a shine!"

"I know your tricks, mariachi!" She glared at Miguel. "What did he say to you?"

"He was just showing me his guitar," Miguel said sheepishly. His family gasped.

"Shame on you!" Tío Berto barked at the mariachi. Abuelita's shoe was aimed directly at the area between the musician's eyes.

"My grandson is a sweet little angelito querido cielito—he wants no part of your music, mariachi! You keep away from him!" she threatened. Miguel wasn't so sure he was the sweet little angel from heaven she'd described, but he wasn't going to argue when she was gripping her shoe like that.

The mariachi scampered away, pulling on his hat before leaving. Miguel watched apologetically over his abuelita's shoulder.

"Ay, pobrecito!" Abuelita pulled her grandson protectively to her bosom. "Estás bien, m'ijo?" Miguel gasped for air. "You know better than to be here in this place! You will come home. Now!" she ordered, and turned away from the plaza.

Miguel sighed and gathered his shine box. He spotted a plaza talent-show flyer on the ground. Behind his abuelita's back, he snatched it up and put it in his pocket.

Chapter
2

Miguel trudged home behind his family, carrying an armful of marigolds.

"How many times have we told you—that plaza is crawling with mariachis!" Tío Berto said.

"Yes, Tío Berto," Miguel answered.

A few minutes later, Miguel had dropped off his marigolds and was ushered into the Rivera family's shoe workshop, where he plopped onto a stool. Surrounded by the rhythm of hammering, Miguel braced himself for a stern round of lecturing from the whole family.

"I found your son in Mariachi Plaza!" Abuelita said. Miguel's parents looked up from their work.

"Miguel," Papá said, disappointment in his voice.

"You know how Abuelita feels about the plaza," said Miguel's mother, a hand on her pregnant belly.

"I was just shining shoes!" Miguel replied.

"A musician's shoes!" added Tío Berto, prompting gasps from every corner of the shop. Primo Abel was so shocked that the shoe he was working on zipped away from the polisher and shot up into the ceiling's rafters.

"But the plaza's where all the foot traffic is!" Miguel tried to explain.

"If Abuelita says no more plaza, then no more plaza," said his father.

"What about tonight?" Miguel blurted.

"What's tonight?" his grandpa asked.

"It's Día de los Muertos," Miguel said hesitantly. "The whole town's gonna be there, and . . . well, they're having this talent show—"

"Talent show?" Abuelita said with a tone of suspicion. Miguel squirmed on the stool, unsure whether he should continue.

"And I thought I might . . . ," Miguel stopped. His mamá gave him a curious gaze.

"Sign up?" she asked.

"Well, maybe?" Miguel finished.

Prima Rosa laughed. "You have to have talent to be in a talent show."

"What are you gonna do, shine shoes?" teased Primo Abel.

"It's Día de los Muertos," Abuelita said. "No one's going anywhere. Tonight is about family." She dropped marigolds into Miguel's arms. "Ofrenda room. Vámonos!"

Miguel followed his abuelita to the ofrenda room with the pile of golden blooms. The room was bright and open, dominated by a wall lined with tables and shelves covered with pictures, candles, flowers, and food offerings to the ancestors. Mamá Coco was already there. Miguel pouted as Abuelita arranged the flowers on the shrines.

"Don't give me that look," Abuelita said to Miguel. "It's the one night of the year when our ancestors can visit us. We put their photos on the ofrenda so their spirits can cross over. If we don't put them up, they can't come! We made all this food, m'ijo, and set out the things they loved in life. All this work to bring the family together. I don't want you sneaking off to who knows where." She looked up from the altar just in time to catch Miguel slipping out of the room.

"Where are you going?" she huffed.

"I thought we were done," Miguel said, turning around.

"Ay, Dios mío," she muttered. "Being part of this family means being HERE for this family. I don't want to see you end up like . . ." She gazed up at the photo of Mamá Imelda.

"Like Mamá Coco's papá?"

"Never mention that man!" Abuelita snapped, sliding a sideways glance toward Mamá Coco. "He's better off forgotten."

"But you're the one who—"

"Ta, ta, ta—tch!"

"Papá?" Mamá Coco said suddenly. Abuelita and Miguel turned toward Mamá Coco. She was anxiously looking around the room. "Papá is home?"

"Mamá, cálmese, cálmese," Abuelita said, rushing to comfort her mom.

"Papá is coming home?" Mamá Coco asked again.

"No, Mamá. It's okay, I'm here," Abuelita said. Mamá Coco looked up with a blank stare.

"Who are you?" Mamá Coco asked.

Abuelita's face dropped, but she recovered with a

gentle smile. "Rest, Mamá," she said. She returned to the altar and continued her lecture. "I'm hard on you because I care, Miguel." She stopped and looked around the room. "Miguel? Miguel?" She let out a long sigh when she realized that he'd slipped out. "What are we going to do with that boy?"

Chapter 3

A little later, Dante wriggled into Miguel's attic hideout. Miguel was huddled over a makeshift guitar patched together from an old soundboard and other random items.

Dante squirmed, making noise. Miguel shushed him. "You're gonna get me in trouble," he said. "Someone could hear me!"

Dante peered around Miguel's shoulders as Miguel took a china marker and colored in a gold tooth on his own version of a skull guitar. Now it looked just like Ernesto de la Cruz's famous instrument. "I wish someone *wanted* to hear me," Miguel said, tuning the guitar. "Other than you." Dante responded with a sloppy lick to his face. Miguel lifted his guitar and strummed it. "Perfecto!"

Miguel crawled to the far side of the attic, where he kept his ofrenda to Ernesto de la Cruz. On the altar, he had set up posters, candles, and songbooks. He lit some candles beside an album of Ernesto's. On the cover, the famous crooner smiled and held his equally famous guitar. Miguel quickly compared the head of his guitar to Ernesto's. It was a good match. Then he imitated Ernesto's dramatic pose and wide smile.

He switched on an old, beat-up TV and slid a *Best of Ernesto de la Cruz* videotape into a machine attached to it. The machine hummed as a black-and-white film clip played. A young Ernesto was speaking.

"I have to sing. I have to play. The music, it's . . . it's not just in me. It is *me,"* he said.

Miguel plucked his homemade guitar as another clip played.

"When life gets me down, I play my guitar," Ernesto cooed.

Another clip showed Ernesto speaking to a beautiful woman. *"The rest of the world may follow the rules, but I must follow my heart!"* He kissed her, and Miguel winced.

Another clip cut in.

"You know that feeling?" the singer asked. *"Like there's a song in the air and it's playing just for you?"*

Ernesto began to sing and strum his guitar. Miguel watched closely, copying his hand positions.

Miguel continued to play as clip after clip flashed on the screen, letting his chords intertwine with the music from the films.

"Never underestimate the power of music," Ernesto said.

In the next segment was another beautiful woman who pined for Ernesto. *"But my father, he will never give his permission,"* she said sweetly.

"I am done asking permission!" Ernesto exclaimed. *"When you see your moment, you mustn't let it pass you by. You must seize it!"*

Miguel's heart beat faster. He wanted to seize his moment, just like Ernesto.

"Señor De la Cruz, what did it take for you to seize your moment?" asked a reporter in a new clip.

"I had to have faith in my dream," Ernesto answered. *"No one was going to hand it to me. It was up to me to reach for that dream, grab it tight, and make it come true."*

". . . and make it come true," Miguel said along with Ernesto. He reached into his pocket and pulled out the talent-show flyer. "No more hiding, Dante. I gotta seize my moment!" Dante panted happily and wagged his tail. "I'm gonna play in Mariachi Plaza if it kills me."

Chapter 4

"Día de Los Muertos has begun!" Abuelita announced, opening the gates to the family's home and courtyard. Toddlers scattered marigold petals along the ground.

"No, no, no, no, no," Miguel's mother said to the children. "We have to make a clear path. These petals guide our ancestors home. We don't want them to get lost. We want them to come and enjoy all the food and drinks on the ofrenda, sí?"

The children nodded. As she helped them create a path of marigold petals from the ofrenda room to the front gate, Miguel and Dante scurried across the roof and dropped to the sidewalk outside the family home. Miguel clutched his homemade guitar. In just a few more steps, he wouldn't have to hide! Suddenly,

Tío Berto and Miguel's father rounded the corner, carrying a small table.

With his heart pounding, Miguel backed up toward the hacienda to avoid the adults, only to find his abuelita shaking out a rug behind him. He and Dante ducked into a corner.

"In the courtyard, m'ijos," she said to Papá and Tío Berto.

"You want it down by the kitchen?" Papá asked.

"Sí. Eh . . . next to the other one," she answered.

Miguel and Dante disappeared into the ofrenda room before anyone spotted them. Mamá Coco was inside, resting.

"Get under, get under!" Miguel urged Dante, quickly stashing the dog and the guitar beneath the altar table just as Miguel's parents and Abuelita entered.

"Miguel!" Abuelita exclaimed.

"Nothing!" Miguel said, turning to face her. "Mamá, Papá, I—"

"Miguel," said his papá. "Your abuelita had the most wonderful idea! We've all decided it's time you joined us in the workshop!" He pulled out a leather apron and dropped it on Miguel's shoulders.

"What!" exclaimed Miguel.

"No more shining shoes. You will be MAKING them! Every day after school!"

Abuelita squeezed Miguel's cheeks. "Oh, our Miguelito carrying on the family tradition! And on Día de los Muertos! Your ancestors will be so proud!" She gestured to the shoes adorning the ofrenda. "You'll craft huaraches, just like your Tía Victoria."

"And wingtips like your Papá Julio," said Miguel's father.

Miguel stepped away from the ofrenda. "But what if I'm no good at making shoes?"

"Ah, Miguel!" Papá said. "You have your family here to guide you. You are a Rivera. And a Rivera is—"

"A shoemaker. Through and through," Miguel finished in a monotone voice.

Papá swelled with pride. "That's my boy! Ha, ha! Berto, break out the good stuff; I wanna make a toast!"

Abuelita smothered Miguel with kisses as the adults exited. Miguel stole a look at the ofrenda, where Dante and his guitar were hidden. Miguel was shocked to see Dante eating the ofrenda offerings!

"No, Dante—stop!"

As Miguel pulled the dog away from the ofrenda, the table shook, and the frame holding Mamá Imelda's old photo swayed back and forth. Miguel watched in horror as the frame toppled over and hit the floor with a sickening crack. Miguel rushed to pick it up, but it fell apart, leaving him holding only the photo of Mamá Imelda and Coco. "No, no, no!" he moaned.

Miguel studied the photo and noticed that another part of it had been folded back and hidden. He unfolded it and saw the body of a man who could only be his great-great-grandfather, standing next to Mamá Imelda, holding a skull guitar. The man's face had been torn from the photo. Miguel couldn't believe the coincidence. The guitar was just like Ernesto de la Cruz's!

Miguel gasped. "Ernesto's guitar?"

Just then, Mamá Coco stirred awake. "Papá?" she said. Mamá Coco pointed a crooked finger at the picture in his hand. "Papá?"

Miguel's eyes widened. He stepped closer to her. "Mamá Coco, is your papá Ernesto de la Cruz?"

"Papá! Papá!" she called louder now.

Miguel rushed to his rooftop hideout. He grabbed Ernesto de la Cruz's album from his ofrenda. He examined the guitar on the album cover and compared it to the guitar in Mamá Imelda's photo. It was an exact match! Could it be true?

"Ha, ha!" Miguel exclaimed. He ran to the edge of the roof and proudly hoisted the picture and album cover. "Papá! Papá!" Miguel yelled to his dad in the courtyard below. His parents looked up at him. "It's him! I know who my great-great-grandfather was!"

Miguel's mom gave him a stern look. "Miguel! Get down from there!"

"Mamá Coco's father was Ernesto de la Cruz!"

"What are you talking about?" Miguel's father asked.

Miguel whipped off his shoemaker's apron and struck a pose. "I'm gonna be a musician!"

Chapter 5

Miguel gathered his guitar and all the Ernesto de la Cruz albums he could carry and raced down from the rooftop. His family surrounded him when he reached the courtyard.

Abuelita's eyes darted from the guitar to the albums. "What is all this?" she said. "You keep secrets from your own family?"

"It's all that time he spends in the plaza," Tío Berto said.

"Fills his head with crazy fantasies," Tía Gloria added.

"It's not a fantasy!" Miguel protested. He handed his father the old photograph of Mamá Imelda, Coco, and the unidentified man and pointed to the guitar.

"That man was Ernesto de la Cruz! The greatest musician of all time!"

"We've never known anything about this man. But whoever he was, he still abandoned his family," Miguel's father said. "This is no future for my son."

"But, Papá, you told me to look to the ofrenda. You said my family would guide me! Well, Ernesto de la Cruz IS my family! I'm supposed to play music!"

"Never! That man's music was a curse! I will not allow it!" Abuelita said, raising her voice.

"You will listen to your family. No more music," added Miguel's father.

"Just listen to me play—"

"End of argument," Papá said.

Miguel thought they'd change their minds if they heard him play. He lifted his guitar and prepared to strum, but Abuelita snatched it from his hands. She pointed to the photo. "You want to end up like that man? Forgotten? Left off your family's ofrenda?"

"I don't care if I'm on some stupid ofrenda!" The words burst out before Miguel could stop them. He couldn't take them back, even though he wanted to.

The family gasped. Abuelita's brow hardened. She raised the guitar in the air.

"No!" Miguel cried.

"Mamá," Miguel's dad said just as Abuelita smashed the guitar against the ground.

"There! No guitar, no music," she said.

The entire family was silent as Miguel stared at his guitar, shattered into a hundred pieces on the ground. Miguel couldn't move—he felt like someone had smashed *him* to pieces.

"Oh, come," Abuelita said to Miguel. "You'll feel better after you eat with your family."

"I don't wanna *be* in this family!" Miguel yelled. He grabbed the photo from his father and bolted out of the courtyard, alone.

Miguel raced into the streets of Santa Cecilia. Dante, who was nose-deep in an overturned trash can, heard Miguel's quick feet and ran into Mariachi Plaza after him. Miguel rushed up to a woman in a gazebo.

"I wanna play in the plaza. Like Ernesto de la Cruz! Can I still sign up for the talent show?"

"You got an instrument?" the woman asked.

"No. But—but if I can borrow a guitar—" Miguel stammered.

"Musicians gotta bring their own instruments,"

she said, and turned to walk away. "You find a guitar, kid, and I'll put you on the list."

Miguel frowned. He needed a guitar. His eyes darted around the plaza. There were tons of musicians roaming around, readying themselves for a busy Day of the Dead. He approached every mariachi, hoping for a lucky break, but no one would help him.

Disheartened, Miguel found himself in front of the Ernesto de la Cruz statue. "Great-Great-Grandfather," he said softly. "What am I supposed to do?" His gaze fell on a plaque at the base of the statue that read SEIZE YOUR MOMENT. Miguel looked at the photo in his hand. He moved his thumb to reveal the skull guitar. At that moment, fireworks exploded overhead, illuminating the statue.

Miguel had an idea.

Chapter 6

The cemetery in Santa Cecilia was covered in a sea of candles and flowers. Families gathered at their loved ones' graves to leave treats and decorate their tombs. No tomb was more decorated than the large mausoleum in the center: it belonged to Ernesto de la Cruz.

Miguel arrived at Ernesto's mausoleum and slunk around the side. Dante started barking. "No, no, Dante, stop! Cállate! Shhh!" Miguel looked around and saw baskets of food and treats left on several tombs for the dead to enjoy. He spotted a plate of food on a nearby grave. He grabbed a chicken leg and chucked it. Dante bounded after it.

Miguel peered through the window of Ernesto de

la Cruz's mausoleum. Inside, he saw what he had come for: Ernesto's famous guitar, mounted on the wall above the tomb. Fireworks continued to explode over the cemetery, and bursts of light glinted off the instrument, as if beckoning Miguel forward. His heart pounded. He knew what he had to do. Timing it with the booming fireworks, Miguel slammed his shoulder against a pane of glass, and opened the window. He crept inside the mausoleum and stepped toward the famous skull guitar. Then he climbed onto the stone tomb to reach it. Now he was face to face with the very instrument that Ernesto de la Cruz had strummed.

"Señor De la Cruz? Please don't be mad. I'm Miguel, your great-great-grandson," Miguel said, glancing up at a painting of Ernesto that hung above the guitar. "I need to borrow this." Miguel lifted the instrument from its mount. Unbeknownst to him, some marigold petals in the mausoleum began to sparkle. "Our family thinks music is a curse. They don't understand, but I know you would've told me to follow my heart. To seize the moment!"

Miguel climbed back down with the guitar clutched protectively under his arm. "So if it's all right with you, I'm gonna play in the plaza, just like you did."

Holding Ernesto's guitar filled Miguel with confidence. He strummed it. With each strum, the air around him vibrated. As he played, all the petals inside the crypt began to glow. Miguel noticed the shimmering petals and froze. What was happening?

Suddenly, a flashlight appeared in the window of the mausoleum. Miguel heard voices outside raising an alarm.

"The guitar! It's gone! Somebody stole Ernesto de la Cruz's guitar!" said one man. "Look! The window's broken."

Miguel froze as keys jingled and the mausoleum door was opened. A groundskeeper entered with a flashlight.

Miguel dropped the guitar. "I'm—I'm sorry!" he stammered. "It's not what it looks like! Ernesto is my—"

The groundskeeper ignored him. Miguel watched as the man approached—then walked straight through him as if he weren't there! Miguel stood there, shocked. How was that man able to pass through him like he was a ghost?

The groundskeeper picked up Ernesto's guitar.

"There's nobody here!" he yelled to the others.

Miguel was scared and confused. He examined his hands, touched his face. Everything was there. Why couldn't the man see him?

Chapter 7

Miguel panicked and sprinted across the cemetery. As he weaved around the crowds, more people passed through him as if he were made of air. Finally, he heard his mother calling him.

"Miguel!" she shouted. Miguel followed her voice.

"Mamá!" Miguel yelled, and reached for her, but she went straight through him, just like the others. They couldn't see or hear him. Miguel tripped and fell into an open grave.

"Dios mío!" a woman shrieked. "Little boy, are you okay?" She reached into the grave. "Here, let me help you."

Miguel took her hand. Finally, someone could see him! She pulled him out of the hole he'd fallen into.

"Thanks, I—" Miguel said, and then stopped. He looked at his rescuer. She was a skeleton! Miguel screamed. The skeleton woman screamed, too! Miguel stumbled and scooted backward, trying to get as far away from the woman as he could. He bumped into another skeleton—whose head fell off. *Plop!* It landed in Miguel's hands. He yelped.

"Do you mind?" said the headless skeleton.

Miguel turned the skull around in his hands to see its face.

"Ahhhh!" screamed the bodyless skull.

"Ahhhh!" Miguel shrieked back. He flung the skeleton head away. Then he looked around to see that the whole cemetery was teeming with skeletons. And they could see him! Miguel's eyes widened as the skeletons stared back at him.

Miguel raced off and crouched behind a grave. From a safe distance, he watched as the skeletons danced and enjoyed the food that had been left for them on the gravestones. Miguel couldn't believe it! Somehow he could see walking, talking skeletons!

A skeleton abuela gazed at her living toddler grandchild. "Look how big she's getting!" she said proudly. Like the other living people, the toddler's family was there to pay respects to their ancestors.

"It's a dream. I'm just dreaming," Miguel muttered. Suddenly, Dante appeared. The silly dog surprised Miguel with a long lick on the cheek.

"Dante? You can see me? W-wait, what's going on?" Miguel stuttered. Dante barked, then darted through the crowd. "Dante!" He chased the dog until—*BAM!* He ran into a mustached skeleton and knocked him to the ground. The skeleton's bones separated and scattered everywhere.

"I'm sorry, I'm sorry," Miguel said as he scrambled to pick up the bones.

The skeleton spoke. "Miguel?"

"Miguel?" another skeleton said.

Miguel looked up. Was he supposed to know these skeletons?

"You're here! *HERE!*" the first skeleton exclaimed as his bones magically pulled themselves back together. "And you can see us!"

Miguel stood and tried to concentrate on their skeletal faces.

A skeleton woman charged through the group, sending bones scattering everywhere again. She grabbed Miguel by the arms. "Our Miguelito!" she said, pulling him into a tight hug.

"Remind me how I know you?" Miguel managed

to ask, certain he'd never seen them before.

"We're your *family*, m'ijo!" she answered him.

Tía Rosita's ofrenda photo flashed in his mind. "Tía Rosita?" he said, still unsure. He looked over at the skeleton man whose head was still turned the wrong way. Tía Victoria straightened it. "Papá Julio? Tía Victoria?"

"He doesn't seem entirely dead," said Tía Victoria, pinching Miguel's cheek. She could tell he wasn't a skeleton like them.

"He's not quite alive, either," added Tía Rosita. Miguel's ancestors looked around, confused.

"We need Mamá Imelda," said Papá Julio. "She'll know how to fix this."

Suddenly, two skeletons came running up. Miguel recognized them as Tío Óscar and Tío Felipe.

"Oy!" shouted Tío Felipe.

"It's Mamá Imelda—" said Tío Óscar.

The twins continued to explain:

"She couldn't cross over—"

"She's stuck—"

"—on the other side."

Tía Victoria narrowed her eyes at Miguel. "I have a feeling this has something to do with you."

"If Mamá Imelda can't come to us—" began Tía Rosita.

"Then WE are going to HER!" exclaimed Papá Julio. "Vámonos!"

Chapter 8

Miguel followed his deceased family as they weaved through the graves in the cemetery and rounded a corner toward a glowing bridge.

"Whoa," Miguel said, slowing down to take in the view of the shimmering structure. It was made from glowing marigolds and extended into a smoky mist.

"Come on, Miguel. It's okay," Papá Julio said as they joined a stream of skeletons ambling across the bridge. With each step Miguel took, the marigold petals glowed beneath his feet. He bent to scoop a bunch of petals into his hands. Suddenly, Dante rushed past him.

"Dante! Dante!" Miguel yelled after him. "Dante, wait up!" He finally caught up with his dog at the crest of the bridge. Dante rolled around in the petals and sneezed into Miguel's face. "You gotta stay with me, boy. We don't know where . . ." Miguel stopped, gazing at the sparkling cityscape of an unreal world before him. The night sky twinkled gold, purple, and yellow. Houses and large buildings were brightly lit and connected by intricate arching bridges. It was the Land of the Dead, but it was very much alive.

"This isn't a dream, then," Miguel said as his family finally reached him. "You're all really out there."

"You thought we weren't?" said Tía Victoria, sounding a bit hurt.

"Well, I don't know. I thought it might've been one of those made-up things that adults tell kids . . . like vitamins."

"Miguel, vitamins are a real thing," Tía Victoria replied.

"Well, now I'm thinking maybe they could be . . . ," Miguel said, moving along with his family. As skeletons passed in the opposite direction, many of them gave Miguel strange looks.

"He looks funny, Mamá," a little skeleton girl said, pointing at Miguel.

"M'ija, it's not nice to stare at—" The little girl's mother stopped in shock when she caught a glimpse of Miguel. "Ay! Santa Maria!" The woman went wide-eyed, her head turning backward to keep staring at Miguel as she walked in the opposite direction. Miguel pulled up his hood to hide the fact that he was still a living, breathing boy.

Soon they reached a large building on the far side of the bridge. Miguel noticed colorful, fantastical creatures crawling, flying, and making nests in the architecture. He pointed up at them. "Are those alebrijes?" They looked just like the wooden figurines in Santa Cecilia. "But those are—"

"REAL alebrijes," said Tío Óscar. "Spirit creatures."

"They guide souls on their journey to the Land of the Dead," said Tía Rosita.

"Watch your step," Tío Felipe added. "They make caquitas everywhere."

Miguel slowed, keeping an eye out for alebrije droppings.

Inside the station, a greeting boomed from the speakers above them. "Welcome back to the Land of the Dead. Please have all offerings ready for reentry. We hope you enjoyed your holiday."

Miguel's eyes darted around the station. He was fascinated by the bustling throngs of dead families and couples lined up under a sign that read REENTRY.

"Welcome back! Anything to declare?" an arrivals agent asked a skeleton.

"Some churros from my family," said the traveler.

"How wonderful!" The agent turned to the next skeleton. "Next! Anything to declare?"

Again, an announcement boomed overhead. "If you are experiencing travel issues, agents at the Department of Family Reunions are available to help you."

Miguel followed his family to find their place in line for arrivals.

While waiting, Miguel watched as skeletons exited the Land of the Dead through another gate marked DEPARTURES.

"Next family, please!" a departures agent called out. An elderly couple stepped in front of a camera-mounted monitor. The monitor scanned their faces and displayed an image of their photos on an altar in the Land of the Living. "Oh, your photos are on your son's ofrenda. Have a great visit!"

"Gracias," said the elderly couple, who then met the rest of their family at the edge of the bridge.

"And remember to return before sunrise," continued the announcement loop. "Enjoy your visit!"

"Next family!" shouted the departures agent. A skeleton with a wide smile full of metal braces stepped up to the monitor. "Your photo's on your dentist's ofrenda. Enjoy your visit!"

"Grashiash!" said the smiling skeleton.

"Next!" the agent called out. A woman dressed in a colorful frock, with flowers pinned in her hair and a dark unibrow above her eyes, stepped up.

"Yes, it is I. Frida Kahlo," the artist said, pointing gracefully at herself. "Famous Mexican icon, beloved of the people. Shall we skip the scanner? I'm on so many ofrendas, it'll just overwhelm your blinky thingie. . . ."

The machine scanned the artist, but the monitor displayed a large X. An alarm blared. "Well, shoot," said the agent. "Looks like no one put up your photo, Frida."

The artist ripped off her unibrow and threw off her frock. They could see that this was not the famous artist, but a young man instead.

"Okay, when I said I was Frida . . . just now? That was a lie," the young man said. "And I apologize for doing that."

"No photo on ofrenda, no crossing the bridge," the agent warned.

"You know what, I'm just gonna zip right over. You won't even know I'm gone." The man bolted for the bridge.

A security guard blocked the gate, but the man split himself in two and slid past, half of him going over, the other half under. He reached the bridge at a sprint and tried to step onto it, but he slowly sank into the petals. It was just as the agent had said: without a photo on an ofrenda, the bridge wouldn't let him cross.

"Almost there . . . Just a little farther . . . ," he mumbled, forcing himself through the thick flowers.

The security guards sauntered over to the bridge and pulled the man back to the Land of the Dead.

"Upsy-daisy," said an officer.

"Fine, okay. Fine, who cares! Dumb flower bridge!"

The guards hauled him away. Tía Rosita looked up just in time to see his back.

"Oh, so sad. I don't know what I'd do if no one put up my photo," she said, shaking her head.

"Next!" an arrivals agent shouted to Miguel's family.

"Oh! Come, m'ijo, it's our turn," Tía Rosita said to Miguel, guiding him forward. The family crowded around the gate. An agent leaned out his window.

"Welcome back, amigos! Anything to declare?"

"As a matter of fact, yes," says Papá Julio. The family pushed Miguel to the front.

Miguel pulled back his hood to reveal himself as a living boy. "Hola," he said.

The agent looked up, and his jawbone dropped—to the floor.

Chapter
9

A security guard escorted Miguel and his family to Marigold Grand Central Station. Dante happily trotted alongside Miguel. The family reached the end of the walkway and passed through a large door emblazoned with DEPARTMENT OF FAMILY REUNIONS.

Inside, hundreds of caseworkers sat in front of computers at cubicles, helping travelers solve holiday snafus.

"C'mon! Help us out, amigo. We gotta get to a dozen ofrendas tonight," one traveler complained.

In a far corner of the room, a woman's voice boomed.

"My family always—ALWAYS—puts my photo on the ofrenda! That devil box tells you nothing but lies!" In one swift movement, she removed her shoe and smacked her caseworker's computer.

"Mamá Imelda?" Papá Julio said. She turned her shoe on him. He stepped back and yelped.

"Oh, mi familia!" she said, her voice softening. "Tell this woman and her devil box that my photo is on the ofrenda."

"Well, we never made it to the ofrenda—" Papá Julio began to explain before Mamá Imelda interrupted.

"What!"

"We ran into um . . . um . . ."

Mamá Imelda's eyes fell on Miguel. He looked at her.

"Miguel!" she gasped.

"Mamá Imelda," Miguel said.

"What is going on?" she asked.

Just then, a door opened and a clerk poked his head in. "You the Rivera family?"

Inside the clerk's office, the Riveras waited for the clerk to explain the situation. He flipped through the accordion folds of a massive printout.

"Well, you're cursed," he said to Miguel. The entire family gasped.

"What!" Miguel exclaimed.

"Día de los Muertos is a night to GIVE to the dead. You STOLE from the dead."

"But I wasn't stealing the guitar!" Miguel protested, shooting pleading looks at his family.

"Guitar?" Mamá Imelda asked with suspicion.

"It was my great-great-grandfather's. He would have wanted me to have it—"

"Ah-ah-ah!" Mamá Imelda interrupted Miguel. "We do not speak of that . . . musician! He is DEAD to this family!"

"Uh, you're all dead," Miguel pointed out.

Dante balanced his paws at the edge of the clerk's desk and tried to reach a bowl of sugary treats.

"*Achoo!*" The clerk sneezed. "I am sorry—whose alebrije is that?" he asked.

Miguel stepped up and tried to pull his dog away from the man's desk "That's just Dante," he answered.

"He sure doesn't look like an alebrije," said Tía Rosita, gesturing to the fantastical creatures fluttering on the other side of the window.

"He just looks like a plain old dog," said Tío Óscar.

"Or a sausage someone dropped in a barbershop," joked Tío Felipe.

45

"Whatever he is, I am—*ACHOO!*—terribly allergic," said the clerk.

"But Dante doesn't have any hair," Miguel said.

"And I don't have a nose, and yet here we are—" The clerk sneezed again.

"But none of this explains why I couldn't cross over," said Mamá Imelda.

Miguel thought back to his family's ofrenda room. He sheepishly pulled the black-and-white photo from his pocket. "Oh," he said, and unfolded the photo of Mamá Imelda, Mamá Coco, and the unidentified man.

"You took my photo off the ofrenda?" Mamá Imelda exclaimed.

"It was an accident!" Miguel said.

Mamá Imelda turned to the clerk with urgency. "How do we send him back?"

"Well, since it's a family matter"—the clerk flipped through the pages of a reference book—"the way to undo a family *curse* is to get your family's *blessing*."

"That's it?" Miguel said.

"Get your family's blessing, and everything *should* go back to normal. But you gotta do it by sunrise," warned the clerk.

"What happens at sunrise?" Miguel asked.

"Híjole!" Papá Julio suddenly exclaimed. "Your hand!"

Miguel looked. The tip of one of his fingers had started to turn skeletal. Miguel paled and began to faint, but Papá Julio caught him and slapped him awake.

"Whoa, Miguel," said Papá Julio. "Can't have you fainting on us!" They had no time to waste. Miguel would turn fully skeletal by sunrise.

The clerk stepped over. "But not to worry! Your family's here; you can get their blessing right now." He knelt next to Tía Rosita and searched the hem of her skirt.

"Cempasúchil . . . cempasúchil," he said, looking for a flower. "Aha! Perdón, señora." He plucked a marigold petal from her dress and handed it to Mamá Imelda. "Now," he went on, "you look at the living and say his name."

Mamá Imelda faced Miguel. "Miguel," she said.

"Nailed it! Now say 'I give you my blessing.'"

"I give you my blessing," Mamá Imelda repeated. The marigold petal glowed in her fingers.

Miguel suddenly felt relieved. He was going home, and he was going to play in the talent show—but Mamá Imelda wasn't finished.

"I give you my blessing to go home . . . ," she continued. The glow surged higher. "To put my photo back on the ofrenda . . ." Miguel nodded as the petal's glow surged higher with each condition. "And to never play music again!" The petal surged one final time.

"What? She can't do that!" Miguel protested.

"Well, technically she can add any conditions she wants," said the clerk.

Miguel narrowed his eyes at her. Mamá Imelda stared back, firm in her resolve.

"Fine," Miguel said.

"Then you hand the petal to Miguel," said the clerk.

Mamá Imelda extended the petal to Miguel. He grasped it. *Whoosh!* He was consumed by a whirlwind of petals, and then he disappeared.

As quickly as he had vanished from the Land of the Dead, he reappeared in Ernesto de la Cruz's mausoleum in a swirl of petals. As soon as the petals settled, Miguel ran to the window and looked out. "No skeletons!" he exclaimed, laughing. Then he saw Ernesto's guitar. Once again, he snatched it from its mount. "Mariachi Plaza, here I come!" He took two steps toward the door, and *whoosh!*

In another whirlwind of petals, Miguel appeared back at the clerk's office in the Land of the Dead. His family turned, shocked to see him back so soon. Miguel realized that his hands were still positioned as if he were holding Ernesto de la Cruz's guitar, though the guitar had stayed in the Land of the Living. Apparently, Mamá Imelda's conditions were enforceable.

"Two seconds, and you already break your promise!" scolded Mamá Imelda.

"This isn't fair—it's my life! You already had yours!" Miguel said. He grabbed another petal. "Papá Julio, I ask for *your* blessing." Papá Julio glanced at Mamá Imelda, whose brow hardened. Intimidated, he shook his head and pulled his hat down. Miguel looked at his other relatives. "Tía Rosita? Óscar? Felipe? Tía Victoria?" They all shook their heads. None of them dared to cross Mamá Imelda.

"Don't make this hard, m'ijo. You go home my way or no way," Mamá Imelda said.

"You really hate music that much?" Miguel asked.

"I will not let you go down the same path he did," she answered. Miguel pulled out the photo. He focused on the man, his great-great-grandfather, whose face had been torn from the photo.

"The same path he did," Miguel whispered to himself, looking at the man. "He's family. . . ."

"Listen to your Mamá Imelda," Tía Victoria pleaded.

"She's just looking out for you," said Tío Óscar.

"Be reasonable," Tía Rosita added.

Miguel slowly stepped toward the door. "Con permiso, I need to visit the restroom. Be right back!" He showed himself out.

The family watched Miguel leave, bewildered. The clerk glanced over at them.

"Uh, should we tell him there are no restrooms in the Land of the Dead?" he said.

Chapter
10

Miguel hustled down a staircase with Dante following him. Once they reached the ground floor, they huddled beneath the stairs. He looked up and saw his family on the upper floor searching for him. Tío Óscar was speaking to a patrolwoman. After a few seconds, she picked up her walkie-talkie.

Miguel scoped the ground floor, quickly spotting a revolving-door exit. "Vámonos," Miguel said to Dante, and pulled his hood up to cover his head. Dante padded after him toward the exit. "If I wanna be a musician, I need a musician's blessing. We gotta find my great-great-grandpa." Miguel was within feet of the exit when a patrolman stepped in front of him.

"Hold it, muchacho."

Miguel spun around so quickly that his hoodie loosened to reveal his living face.

"Ahh!" screamed the patrolman. Miguel tried to pass him but couldn't.

Then a patrolwoman's voice spoke on his walkie-talkie: "Uh, we got a family looking for a living boy." The patrolman exchanged a look with Miguel.

"I got him," he answered.

Suddenly, a large, chatty family with their arms full of offerings passed between Miguel and the patrolman.

"Uh—whoa, excuse me, excuse me, folks!" the patrolman stammered as he tried to avoid bumping into the family.

Miguel used the distraction to escape. He and Dante zipped down a corridor, but Dante doubled back to inspect a side room.

"Dante!" Miguel shouted. He followed Dante into a room marked DEPARTMENT OF CORRECTIONS. Miguel overheard two men talking as he tried to grab his dog.

". . . disturbing the peace, fleeing an officer, falsifying a unibrow . . ."

"That's illegal?" another man asked in disbelief.

"VERY illegal. You need to clean up your act, amigo," said the corrections officer.

"Amigo?" the young man repeated softly. "That's so nice to hear you say that, because I've just had a really hard Día de los Muertos, and I could really use an amigo right now."

"Uh," said the corrections officer.

"And amigos, they help their amigos. Listen, you get me across that bridge tonight and I'll make it worth your while," the young man said. He spotted an Ernesto de la Cruz poster in the officer's workstation. "Oh, you like Ernesto? He and I go way back! I can get you front-row seats to his Sunrise Spectacular show."

Miguel perked up at the mention of Ernesto de la Cruz.

"I'll—I'll get you backstage. You can meet him!" the young man said. "You just gotta let me cross that bridge!"

The corrections officer shook his head, rejecting the offer. "I should lock you up for the rest of the holiday," he threatened. "But my shift's almost up, and I wanna visit my living family, so I'm letting you off with a warning."

"Can I at least get my costume back?" The young man pointed to his Frida Kahlo outfit.

"Uh, no."

In a huff, the ragged young man marched out of the room. "Some amigo," he scoffed.

Miguel followed him into the hallway. "Hey! Hey! You really know Ernesto de la Cruz?"

"Who wants to kno—" the man said, and then stopped in shock once he got a good look at Miguel. "Ah, ay! You're alive!"

"Shhh!" Miguel said. He quickly yanked the young man into a phone booth to avoid a scene. "Yeah, I'm alive. And if I wanna get back to the Land of the Living, I need Ernesto de la Cruz's blessing."

"That's weirdly specific."

"He's my great-great-grandfather."

"He's your gr-gr— Wh-whaaat?" The man's jaw dropped. Miguel caught it just before it landed on the floor, then pushed it back into place. "Wait!" the skeleton said. "You're going back to the Land of the Living?"

Miguel stepped back, unsure. "Ya know what, maybe this isn't such a great—"

The man snapped his fingers rapidly. "No, niño, I can help you! You can help me. We can help each other! But most importantly, you can help ME!"

Suddenly, Miguel spotted his family coming down a staircase. Mamá Imelda saw Miguel and barreled straight for him. "Miguel!" she shouted.

Miguel couldn't let them catch him and send him back to the Land of the Living with a hundred conditions to never play music.

Unaware that Miguel's family was closing in, the skeleton extended his hand. "I'm Hector."

"That's nice," Miguel said, gripping Hector by the wrist and dragging him to the exit. Miguel and Dante burst out the door and sped down the stairs. At the bottom of the stairs, Miguel realized he was holding only Hector's arm. The rest of the skeleton was missing.

"Espérame, chamaco!" Hector yelled, trying to get Miguel to slow down.

Miguel looked around. His family was stuck in a revolving door. Moments later, they emerged and scoured the area. But Miguel was gone.

"Ay!" Mamá Imelda cried. "He is going to get himself killed. We need Pepita."

She brought two fingers to her mouth and whistled. A shadow whooshed over them, and then a giant winged jaguar landed in front of the family.

Her wings glowed green and blue, and her eyes were bright in the night.

"Who has that petal he touched?" asked Mamá Imelda.

Papá Julio held it out to Pepita. "Nice alebrije . . ."

Pepita focused on the scent and, moments later, took to the sky.

Chapter 11

In a dark alley, Miguel sat still on a wooden crate. Hector hovered over him with an open can of black shoe polish. He smudged a thumb bone across the boy's face.

"Hey, hey, hold still, hold still. Look up. Look up. UP! Ta-da!" Hector said after painting Miguel's face to resemble a skeleton. "Dead as a doorknob." Hector and Miguel exchanged satisfied grins. "So listen, Miguel. This place runs on memories. When you're well remembered, people put up your photo and you get to cross the bridge and visit the living on Día de los Muertos. Unless you're me."

"You don't get to cross over?" Miguel asked.

"No one's ever put up my picture. But you can change that!" He unfolded an old picture and showed it to Miguel. In the photo was a young, living Hector.

"This is you?"

"Muy guapo, eh?"

"So you get me to my great-great-grandpa, then I put up your photo when I get home?"

"Such a smart boy! Yes! Great idea, yes!" Hector said. "One hiccup—Ernesto de la Cruz is a tough guy to get to, and I need to cross that bridge soon. Like, TONIGHT. So, you got any other family here? You know, someone a bit more . . . eh, accessible?"

"Mmmmm, nope."

"Don't yank my chain, chamaco. You gotta have SOME other family."

"ONLY Ernesto. Listen, if you can't help me, I'll find him myself," Miguel said, then whistled for his dog. "C'mon Dante." He marched out of the alley, Dante loyally following behind.

"Ugh, okay, okay, kid, fine—fine! I'll get you to your great-great-grandpa!"

Hector led Miguel out of the alley and into a crowded street. "It's not gonna be easy, you know? He's a busy man," said Hector.

A large billboard advertising an Ernesto de la Cruz concert stopped Miguel in his tracks. Ernesto's biggest hit song, "Remember Me," blared from some speakers.

"Ernesto de la Cruz's Sunrise Spectacular!" Miguel exclaimed.

"Blech! Every year, your great-great-grandpa puts on that dumb show to mark the end of Día de los Muertos."

"And you can get us in!"

"Ahhhhhh . . ."

"Hey, you said you had front-row tickets!" Miguel said.

"That . . . that was a lie. I apologize."

Miguel gave Hector a withering look.

"Cool off, chamaco. Come on, I'll get you to him."

"How?"

"'Cause I happen to know where he's rehearsing."

Chapter
12

Hector and Miguel arrived in front of a large warehouse. Hector detached his arm and used his suspenders to sling it toward a third-floor window. His hand tapped on it. Inside, a seamstress turned away from a costume and looked. The hand waved at her. She rolled her eyes and went to let them in.

"You better have my dress, Hector!" she yelled down.

"Hola, Ceci!" Hector said, all smiles. Hector reattached his arm as she lowered a fire-escape ladder so they could come up.

"Hola," Miguel said, tumbling through the window.

"Ceci, I lost the dress—" Hector began.

As Ceci started to yell at him about her Frida costume, Dante wandered away.

"Dante," Miguel said, following him to a big stage where performers were rehearsing. "We shouldn't be in here. . . ." His dog sniffed around. Suddenly, a spirit-guide monkey jumped out at Dante and leapt onto the dog's back. He rode poor Dante like he was in a rodeo.

"No, no, Dante! Ven acá!" Miguel said, hustling after his dog.

The monkey suddenly jumped onto someone's shoulder. It was Frida Kahlo. The real one—not somebody in a costume. She stood in front of the stage. Miguel reined Dante in just as she noticed them.

"You! How did you get in here?" she said, her unibrow cocked.

"I just followed my—" Miguel began to explain when Frida's eyes widened at the sight of Dante.

"Oh, the mighty Xolo dog! Guider of wandering spirits!" Frida exclaimed, gazing at Dante. "And whose spirit have you guided to me?" She took a closer look at Miguel.

"I don't think he's a spirit guide," Miguel answered.

"Ah-ah-ah," she cautioned. "The alebrijes of *this* world can take many forms. They are as mysterious as they are powerful."

Suddenly, the colorful patterns on Frida's monkey swirled. He opened his mouth to breathe blue fire. That's powerful, Miguel thought. Maybe Dante is special. They looked at the dog, who was busily chewing on his own leg.

Unimpressed, Frida looked back to Miguel. "Or maybe he's just a dog. Come! I need your eyes!"

Frida guided him to the front of the stage to watch a rehearsal.

"You are the audience," she said to Miguel. "Darkness. And from the darkness . . . a giant papaya!" The stage lights zoomed in on a giant papaya prop. "Dancers emerge from the papaya, and the dancers are all me." Unibrowed dancers in leotards crawled around the giant papaya. "And they go to drink from the milk of their mother, who is a cactus but also me. And her milk is not milk, but tears." Frida paused. She glanced over at Miguel. "Is it too obvious?"

"I think it's just the right amount of obvious," Miguel said. "It could use some music, like *doonk-doonk-doonk-doonk.*"

Frida snapped at the musicians, who started playing a discordant pizzicato.

"Oh!" Miguel said with delight. "And then it could

go *dittle-ittle-dittle-ittle-dittle-ittle-dittle-ittle—whaa!*"
The violins followed Miguel's direction.

"And what if everything was on fire?" Frida asked excitedly. "Yes! Fire everywhere!"

The performers gasped and exchanged concerned looks.

"Inspired!" Frida said. She leaned in closer to Miguel. "You! You have the spirit of an artist!" Miguel stood up straighter, letting Frida's words lift him. He wished his family could see what Frida saw in him. He WAS an artist. Not a shoemaker. Frida turned her focus back to the rehearsal. "Dancers exit, the music fades, the lights go out. And Ernesto de la Cruz rises to the stage!" A silhouette rose from a trapdoor in the floor. Miguel leaned forward.

"Ernesto!" he exclaimed. A spotlight shone on the silhouette, revealing it to be a mannequin. "Huh?"

Frida continued to instruct the stage performers. "He does a couple of songs, the sun rises, everyone cheers—"

Miguel was confused. "Excuse me," he said, "where's the real Ernesto de la Cruz?"

"Ernesto doesn't DO rehearsals," Frida said. "He's too busy hosting that fancy party at the top of his tower." She gestured out a large window to a grand tower lit up in the distance, atop a steep hill.

Suddenly, Hector rounded the corner. "Chamaco! You can't rush off on me like that! C'mon, stop pestering the celebrities."

Hector pulled him away, but Miguel resisted.

"You said my great-great-grandpa would be here! He's halfway across town, throwing some big party."

"That bum! Who doesn't show up to his own rehearsal?"

"If you're such good friends, how come he didn't invite you?" Miguel asked.

Hector turned to the musicians. "Hey, Gustavo! You know anything about this party?"

"It's the hot ticket. But if you're not on the guest list, you're never getting in, Chorizo . . . ," he said, sending the musicians into a bout of chuckles.

"Ha, ha! Very funny, guys. Very funny," Hector said back. They continued to heckle him.

"Chorizo?" Miguel asked.

"Oh, this guy's famous!" Gustavo said to Miguel. "Go on, go on—ask him how he died!"

Miguel looked to Hector, curious.

"I don't want to talk about it," Hector said.

"He choked on some chorizo!" Gustavo said, letting

out a raucous laugh along with the other musicians. Miguel couldn't help laughing a little, too.

"I didn't choke, okay—I got food poisoning!" Hector snapped. "Which is a big difference!" The musicians laughed even more. Hector turned to Miguel. "This is why I don't like musicians: a bunch of self-important jerks!"

"Hey, I'm a musician," Miguel protested.

"You are?" asked Hector.

"Well," said Gustavo, "if you really want to get to Ernesto, there IS that music competition at the Plaza de la Cruz. Winner gets to play at his party."

"Music competition?" Miguel asked. He quickly examined his hands to check on his skeletal transformation. It had spread to another finger. He was running out of time.

"No, no, no, chamaco, you are loco if you think—" Hector began.

"I need to get my great-great-grandfather's blessing," Miguel interrupted. He looked up at Hector. "You know where I can get a guitar?"

Hector sighed. "I know a guy."

Above the Land of the Dead, a shadowy figure glided across the sky and landed in a darkened corner of an alley. It sniffed out the canister of shoe polish that Hector had used on Miguel's face. The spirit guide released a low growl.

"Have you found him, Pepita? Have you found our boy?" Mamá Imelda asked, following the large cat with the rest of the family. Pepita breathed onto the ground, magically illuminating a footprint. It glowed for a moment.

"A footprint!" Tía Rosita announced. The whole family leaned in to inspect.

"It's a Rivera boot!" Papá Julio exclaimed.

"Size seven . . . ," said Tío Óscar.

". . . and a half!" finished Tío Felipe.

"Pronated," added Tía Victoria, with her expert eye.

"Miguel," Mamá Imelda said softly.

Pepita leaned forward and breathed again, and the glow spread across a trail of footprints leading into the street.

Chapter 13

Miguel followed Hector down a steep stairway. "So why the heck would you want to be a musician?" asked Hector.

Miguel was offended. "My great-great-grandpa was a musician."

"Who spent his life performing like a monkey for complete strangers. Blech, no thank you, no," Hector said.

"Whadda YOU know?" asked Miguel. "How far is this guitar, anyway?"

"We're almost there." Hector jumped from a stairway to the ground, and his bones scattered, then reassembled. "Keep up, chamaco, come on!"

The stairway in front of them opened up to a small section of town covered in dust. The shimmering brightness that lit up the Land of the Dead seemed to have skipped this area. Miguel gazed at passersby. They were dusty and drab like Hector, lacking the bright decorations and clothing of the Rivera ancestors. A group of dingy skeletons huddled around a burning trash can and laughed raucously. They saw Hector.

"Cousin Hector!" the group hollered.

"Ay! These guys!" Hector said with a big smile. He nodded to a man playing a jaunty tune on a violin made of coffee cans, twine, and other scraps. "Hey, Tío!" Hector called to the man playing the violin.

"These people are all your family?" asked Miguel.

"Eh, in a way. We're all the ones with no photos on ofrendas. No family to go home to. Nearly forgotten, you know?" Hector said with a hint of sadness. "So we all call each other cousin, or tío, or whatever."

Hector and Miguel approached three old ladies playing cards around a wooden crate.

"Hector!" one called out.

"Tía Chelo! Hey, hey!" Hector greeted the old woman. "Is Chicharrón around?"

"In the bungalow. I don't know if he's in the mood for visitors," Tía Chelo said.

"Who doesn't like a visit from Cousin Hector?"

Hector teased as he entered a tent. He held the curtains open for Miguel and Dante to enter. Inside, it was cramped, dark, and quiet. There were stacks of old dishes, a drawer full of pocket watches, and piles of magazines and records stacked high. Miguel stumbled and almost knocked one stack over.

Hector spotted a hammock piled with old trinkets and a dusty hat. He lifted the hat and found the grumpy face of his friend Chicharrón.

"Buenas noches, Chicharrón!"

"I don't wanna see your stupid face, Hector!"

"C'mon, it's Día de los Muertos! I brought you a little offering!"

"Get out of here. . . ."

"I would, Cheech, but the thing is . . . me and my friend here, Miguel, we really need to borrow your guitar."

"My guitar?" Chicharrón shifted in his hammock.

"I promise we'll bring it right back," Hector said. Chicharrón sat up, incensed.

"Like that time you promised to bring back my van?"

"Uh," Hector said.

"Or my mini fridge?"

"Ah, you see . . . uhhhh . . ."

"Or my good napkins? My lasso? My *femur*?"

"No, not like those times."

"Where's my femur? You—" Chicharrón raised a finger to give Hector a tongue-lashing, but then he weakened and collapsed on his hammock, a golden flicker flashing through his bones.

"Whoa, whoa, you okay, amigo?" Hector said, rushing to his friend's side.

Chicharrón let out a long sigh. "I'm fading, Hector. I can feel it." He gazed over at his guitar. "I couldn't even play that thing if I wanted to."

Hector's eyes darted from Chicharrón to the guitar.

"YOU play me something," said Chicharrón.

"Oh, you know I don't play anymore, Cheech," said Hector. "The guitar's for the kid."

"You want it, you got to earn it."

Hector reluctantly reached for the guitar. "Only for you, amigo. Any requests?"

Chicharrón smiled. "You know my favorite, Hector."

Hector grinned and began strumming away on the guitar, playing a lovely, lilting tune. Chicharrón smiled, seeming suddenly at peace. As Hector played, Miguel was amazed. He'd had no idea Hector was a musician—and a good one! The skeleton began to sing a silly song about a woman named Juanita whose knuckles dragged on the floor.

"Those aren't the words!" Chicharrón protested.

"There are children present," Hector said calmly, and continued to sing. He ended the song with a soft flourish.

"Brings back memories," said Chicharrón. "Gracias." Then his eyes closed. Suddenly, the edges of Chicharrón's bones began to glow with a soft, beautiful light. Hector looked sad. Then they watched as Chicharrón dissolved into dust.

"Wait, what happened?" Miguel asked, concerned.

Hector picked up a glass, raised it in honor of Chicharrón, and drank. He put it down next to Chicharrón's glass, which remained full.

"He's been forgotten," Hector said. "When there's no one left in the living world who remembers you, you disappear from this world. We call it the final death."

"Where did he go?" asked Miguel.

"No one knows," said Hector.

Miguel had a thought. "But I've met him. I could remember him, when I go back."

"No, it doesn't work like that, chamaco. Our memories, they have to be passed down by those who knew us in life. In the stories they tell about us. But there's no one left alive to pass down Cheech's stories. . . ."

Miguel fell silent, in deep thought about his family's shrine and keeping their memories alive.

Hector put a hand on Miguel's back, suddenly cheerful. "Hey, it happens to everyone eventually," he said. He gave the guitar to Miguel. "C'mon, de la Cruzcito. You've got a contest to win." Hector slung open the curtain, and Miguel followed Hector out of the tent.

Chapter 14

A little while later, Hector and Miguel were hanging off the back of a moving trolley. Hector fiddled on the guitar idly as they rode through the city.

"You told me you hated musicians. You never said you *were* one," Miguel said.

"How do you think I knew your great-great-grandpa? We used to play music together. Taught him everything he knows." Hector played a fancy riff but botched the last note.

"No manches! You played with Ernesto de la Cruz, the greatest musician of all time?"

"Ha, ha! You're funny!" Hector laughed. "Greatest eyebrows of all time, maybe, but his music? Eh, not so much."

"You don't know what you're talking about," Miguel said.

The trolley reached their stop. "Welcome to Plaza de la Cruz!" Hector announced. In the center of the bustling plaza was a giant statue of Ernesto de la Cruz. "Showtime, chamaco!" Hector pushed the guitar into Miguel's arms.

Miguel looked around the plaza. It glowed and hummed with the shouts of vendors selling a variety of crafts and treats to passersby.

"Llevelo! T-shirts!" called a vendor selling Ernesto de la Cruz souvenirs. "Bobbleheads!"

Miguel gazed past the vendor and saw a large stadium stage, where an emcee was greeting her audience.

"Bienvenidos a todos!" she cried. "Who's ready for some música?" The audience whooped and hollered. "It's a battle of the bands, folks. The winner gets to play for the maestro himself, Ernesto de la Cruz, at his fiesta tonight!" The audience cheered some more. "Let the competition begin!" exclaimed the emcee.

The stage filled with acts performing one after the other. The performers were like none Miguel had ever seen. There was a tuba and violin act, a hardcore metal band, a marimba player on the back of a giant iguana spirit guide, a dog orchestra, and nuns playing accordions.

Miguel and Hector signed up for the contest and headed backstage into a crowd of other performers.

"So what's the plan? What are you gonna play?" Hector asked Miguel.

"Definitely 'Remember Me,'" Miguel answered. He plucked out the beginning notes of the song. Hector clamped his hand over the guitar's fretboard.

"No, not that one. No," Hector said seriously.

"C'mon, it's his most popular song!"

"Eh, it's *too* popular," Hector replied. They gazed around the backstage area and noticed that many other acts were rehearsing their own versions of "Remember Me." One man even played water glasses to the famous tune.

"That song has been butchered enough for a lifetime," Hector said with disgust.

"What about . . ." Miguel thought hard. "'Poco Loco'?"

"Okay! Now you're talking!"

A stagehand approached Miguel. "De la Cruzcito?" he asked. Miguel nodded at his stage name. "You're on standby!" Then the stagehand gestured to another band. "Los Chachalacos, you're up next!"

As Los Chachalacos stepped onto the stage, the crowd roared. The band burst into a mighty intro and the audience went wild.

Backstage, Miguel peeked out at the frenzied audience. Los Chachalacos were unbeatable. He suddenly felt ill. He paced.

"You always this nervous before a performance?" Hector asked.

"I don't know. I've never performed before."

"What? You said you were a musician!"

"I am!" Miguel answered. "I mean, I will be. Once I win."

"That's your plan?" Hector exclaimed. "No, no, no, no, no—you HAVE to win, Miguel. I NEED you to win. Your life LITERALLY depends on you winning AND YOU'VE NEVER DONE THIS BEFORE?"

Miguel processed that. His life *did* depend on him winning. Panic spread across his face.

And Hector saw it. "I'll go up there." He reached for the guitar.

"No!" Miguel said. "I need to do this!"

"Why?" asked Hector.

"If I can't go out there and play ONE song, how can I call myself a musician?"

"What does that matter?"

"'Cause I don't just want to GET Ernesto de la Cruz's blessing. I need to prove that . . . that I'm WORTHY of it."

"Oh," said Hector. "Oh, that's such a sweet sentiment . . . at such a bad time." Then he softened. "Okay, you wanna perform? Then you've got to PERFORM! First, you have to loosen up. Shake off those nerves!" Hector and Miguel did a loose-bone shimmy.

"Now gimme your best grito!" Hector said.

"My best grito?"

"Come on, yell! Belt it out!" Hector said, and then let out a long-throated grito. "Ah, feels good! Okay, now you."

Miguel looked at Hector, uncertain. "A-a-ayyyy-aaaaaaa-yyyyy-ay . . ." Miguel's halting grito was breathy and squeaky.

Dante whimpered.

"Oh, c'mon, kid," Hector said. Behind him on the stage, Los Chachalacos was wrapping up its performance to raucous applause.

"De la Cruzcito, you're on now!" the stagehand called.

"Miguel, look at me," Hector said.

"Come on, let's go!" the stagehand yelled at Miguel, gesturing for him to hit the stage.

"Hey! Hey, look at me," Hector repeated to Miguel to snap him out of his terrified daze. Miguel finally looked up at him. "You can do this. Grab their attention and don't let it go!"

The emcee spoke to the crowd. "We got one more act, amigos," she said.

"Hector," Miguel said softly as the stagehand ushered him to the stage.

"Damas y caballeros! De la Cruzcito!" The emcee shouted.

"Make 'em listen, chamaco! You got this!" Hector called.

Guitar in hand, Miguel stumbled out onto the stage. Blinded by the lights, he squinted at the massive audience. They gazed back at him. Miguel stood there, frozen in fear.

Chapter 15

Hector turned to Dante. "What's he doing? Why isn't he playing?"

Miguel continued to stand stiffly in front of the restless audience, who wanted to dance.

"Bring back the singing dogs!" someone yelled. Miguel looked at Hector, and Hector shimmied. Miguel copied him, took a deep breath, and . . .

"HAAAAAAAI-YAAAAAAAAI-YAAAAAAI-YAAAAAAI!" He let out a full-throated grito.

The audience was stunned. Seconds later, they responded with whistles and whoops. Some returned the grito, while others applauded. Miguel strummed the guitar intro for "Poco Loco," then let his voice carry the lyrics over the jubilant crowd. By the time he had finished the first verse, the audience was on their feet.

Suddenly, Dante grabbed Hector by the leg, trying to pull him onto the stage with Miguel. At first, Hector shook him off, but he finally let Dante drag him out. Once in the spotlight, Hector busted out some percussive footwork to Miguel's guitar.

"Not bad for a dead guy!" Miguel said to Hector.

"You're not so bad yourself, gordito!" Hector said above the exuberant clapping from the audience.

But unbeknownst to Miguel, at the back of the stadium, a ripple of glowing footprints guided Pepita and the Rivera family to the edge of the joyous audience.

"He's close," Mamá Imelda said. "Find him." The family members fanned out, stopping everyone they passed.

"We're looking for a living kid, about twelve," Tío Felipe and Tío Óscar said together.

"Have you seen a living boy?" Tía Rosita prompted.

Although the audience clapped along to the music, Miguel's family paid no attention to the skeleton boy performing onstage, or to the young man next to him, who was becoming more creative with his dance moves. Hector's head bobbed and his limbs spun around. Every new trick made the audience howl with glee.

Hector and Miguel ended their performance with a grito, and the audience erupted into boisterous applause. Miguel smiled, enjoying the moment. He felt like a real musician.

"Hey, you did good!" Hector gushed. "I'm proud of you!"

Miguel's heart swelled. Were they really clapping for him? He looked out at the cheering crowd—and spotted his family. Papá Julio was conversing with the emcee on the other side of the stage!

"Otra! Otra! Otra!" The audience cheered for an encore.

Panicked, Miguel yanked Hector stage left, away from the emcee and Papá Julio. Hector resisted, annoyed that Miguel wasn't going to perform an encore for the audience. "Hey, where are you going?"

"We gotta get out of here," Miguel said, out of breath.

"What, are you crazy? We're about to win this thing!"

"Damas y caballeros, I have an emergency announcement," the emcee said from the stage. The audience quieted. "Please be on the lookout for a living boy, answers to the name of Miguel. Earlier tonight, he ran away from his family. They just want to send him back to the Land of the Living." Murmurs of concern rumbled through the audience. "If anyone has information, please contact the authorities," said the emcee.

Hector eyes widened. "Wait, wait, wait!" He directed his gaze at Miguel. "You said Ernesto de la Cruz was your ONLY family. The ONLY person who could send you home."

"I do have other family, but—" Miguel began to explain.

"You could have taken my photo back this whole time!"

"But they hate music. I need a *musician's* blessing!"

"You lied to me!" Hector said.

"Oh, you're one to talk!"

"Look at me. I'm being forgotten, Miguel. I don't even know if I'm gonna last the night!" Hector said. "I'm not gonna miss my one chance to cross that bridge 'cause you want to live out some stupid musical fantasy!"

"It's not stupid," Miguel said.

Hector grabbed Miguel's arm and pulled him toward the stage. "I'm taking you to your family."

"Let go of me!" Miguel protested, struggling against Hector.

"You'll thank me later—"

Miguel yanked his arm from Hector's grasp. "You don't wanna help me—you only care about yourself! Keep your dumb photo!" He pulled Hector's photo out of his pocket and threw it at him. Hector tried to grab it, but it caught a breeze and drifted into the audience.

"No, no, no!" Hector cried. This was his last chance to be remembered.

"Stay away from me!" Miguel yelled.

As Hector scrambled to get his photo, Miguel ran away. Once Hector had the photo again, he looked around for Miguel.

"Hey, chamaco! Where did you go? Chamaco! I'm sorry! Come back!"

Chapter
16

Dante bounded after Miguel, but looked back at Hector and whimpered. He barked to get Miguel's attention.

"Dante, cállate!" Miguel scolded, but Dante was insistent. He tugged at Miguel's pants, trying to stop him from leaving. "No, Dante! Stop it! He can't help me!" Dante latched on to Miguel's hoodie. Miguel tried to shake Dante off, but instead his hoodie slipped down, revealing the arms of a living boy. Dante redoubled his efforts. "Dante, no, stop! Stop it! Leave me alone! You're not a spirit guide; you're just a dumb dog! Now get out of here!" Miguel yanked his hoodie away from Dante, who shrank back.

The scuffle between the boy and the small dog drew the eyes of the crowd. Startled skeletons saw

Miguel's arms. He hurried to put his hoodie back on as the crowd began to point and shout.

"It's him! It's that living boy!"

"Look! He's alive!"

Miguel ran away and jumped down some scaffolding. In the distance, he could see Ernesto de la Cruz's tower. He dashed ahead, but Pepita landed in front of him, cutting off his path! Miguel skidded to a stop. He screamed when he saw the winged jaguar. Even worse, Mamá Imelda rode atop the feline creature.

"This nonsense ends now, Miguel! I am giving you my blessing, and you are going home!"

"I don't want your blessing!" Miguel shouted, and tried to bolt, but Pepita clutched him with her talons and took to the air. "Ahhh! Put me down! Let go of me!" Miguel twisted his body, grabbing on to a line of papel picado hung high over the audience. He wriggled free from the jaguar's claws, falling back to the ground. Once on his feet, Miguel scrambled upright and ran for a narrow alley staircase.

"Miguel! Stop!" Mamá Imelda called after him in a stern voice. Unable to get through the staircase with Pepita, she continued on foot. "Come back!" Miguel squeezed through an iron gate. Mamá Imelda was stuck on the other side. "I am trying to save your life!"

"You're *ruining* my life!" Miguel yelled back.

"What?" Mamá Imelda froze.

"Music's the only thing that makes me happy. And you—you wanna take that away!" Miguel started up the stairs. "You'll never understand."

A clear, powerful note rang out through the stairwell. Mamá Imelda had begun to sing! Her voice was beautiful and haunting. Miguel stopped.

"I thought you hated music," he said.

"Oh, I loved it," she said. "I remember that feeling when my husband would play, and I would sing, and nothing else mattered." She let out a light laugh. "But when we had Coco, suddenly there was something in my life that mattered more than music. I wanted to put down roots. He wanted to play for the world." She paused, lost in a memory. "We each made a sacrifice to get what we wanted. Now YOU must make a choice."

"But I don't wanna make a choice. I don't wanna pick sides. I want you to pick MY side," Miguel said softly. "That's what family's supposed to do. Support you. But you never will." He wiped the corner of his eyes with the sides of his palms and turned away before Mamá Imelda could answer. Then he climbed the narrow staircase toward Ernesto de la Cruz's tower.

 86

Chapter 17

Miguel arrived at the foot of the hill that led to Ernesto's tower. Limousines, cars, and carriages were lined up, dropping off finely dressed guests. A couple at the front of the line flashed an invitation to a security guard.

"Have a good time," the guard said, guiding them onto a sleek cable car that would take them to Ernesto's mansion at the top of the hill.

Miguel rushed ahead, wriggling between guests to cut to the front of the line.

The security guard stared down at Miguel. "Invitation?"

"It's okay. I'm Ernesto's great-great-grandson!" He struck a dramatic Ernesto de la Cruz signature pose with the guitar.

The security guard flung Miguel through the air and out of the line.

Miguel brushed himself off and spotted Los Chachalacos unloading instruments from a van. They must have won the competition! He darted over to the band. "Disculpen, Señores," Miguel began.

"Hey, hey, guys—it's 'Poco Loco'!" the bandleader said as the other members crowded around, excited to see him.

"You were on fire tonight!" said one band member.

"You too!" Miguel beamed. "Hey, musician to musician—I need a favor."

A few minutes later, the bandleader handed an invitation to the security guard.

"Ooh, the competition winners! Congratulations, chicos!" said the security guard. Los Chachalacos filed onto the tram to the mansion. One member lugged an exceptionally heavy sousaphone. After the tram began its trek upward, he blew on the horn and Miguel came flying out.

Once they arrived at the top, the doors opened to reveal Ernesto de la Cruz's lavish mansion. Miguel and the mariachis filed out.

Miguel gasped at the sight of Ernesto's home. "Whoa," he said.

"Hey, hey!" the bandleader said to Miguel. "Enjoy the party, little músico!"

"Gracias!" Miguel said, and rushed straight inside the mansion to face a lively celebration.

"Look, it's Ernesto!" someone shouted.

Miguel followed the sound of the voice and caught a glimpse of his idol heading deeper into the party. "Ernesto," he said quietly. He pushed through the throngs of people and went up a staircase. He lost his great-great-grandfather in the crowd for a second, but he didn't give up. "Señor de la Cruz! Pardon me, Señor de la Cruz! Señor de la—"

Miguel elbowed his way through guests until suddenly, he was in a huge hall filled with hundreds of partygoers. Synchronized swimmers made formations in a sparkling blue pool while a DJ dropped a mariachi mash-up soundtrack. On the walls, film clips from Ernesto's movies looped continuously. Miguel knew every clip by heart.

One caught his eye. In the clip, a nun was speaking to Ernesto.

"Oh, but, Padre, he will never listen."

"He will listen . . . TO MUSIC!"

Ernesto's fictional words emboldened Miguel. He knew he had to seize the moment. He had to make Ernesto listen and get his blessing. He spotted a pillar that stretched to the landing of a grand staircase and climbed it. Once he stood above the crowd, he took a breath and released the loudest grito he could.

The grito echoed through the space, bouncing off the walls. Every party guest turned toward Miguel, and the DJ faded the music. Feeling everyone's eyes on him, Miguel plucked away at his guitar, singing an introduction. As he sang, a hush fell over the crowd, making his voice and guitar the only sounds in the room. The crowd parted, letting him pass through to reach Ernesto de la Cruz.

Miguel's soul poured into each chord and lyric. He was finally going to meet his idol. He was moving closer and closer, when suddenly—SPLASH!

Miguel tumbled into the pool.

Chapter 18

Ernesto de la Cruz rolled up his sleeves and, in true movie-hero fashion, jumped into the pool. He lifted a coughing Miguel to the edge.

"Are you all right, niño?" Ernesto asked.

Miguel looked up, mortified. The paint on his face began to run, and everyone saw he was a living boy.

Ernesto's eyes widened. The crowd gasped and murmured.

"It's you!" said Ernesto. "You are that boy, the one who came from the Land of the Living."

"Y-you . . . know about me?" Miguel stammered.

"You are all anyone has been talking about! Why have you come here?"

"I'm Miguel. Your great-great-grandson."

The crowd murmured some more. Ernesto leaned back, shocked. "I have a great-great-grandson?"

"I need your blessing. So I can go back home and be a musician, just like you," Miguel said. "The rest of our family, they wouldn't listen. But I . . . I hoped you would."

There was a long pause.

"My boy, with a talent like yours, how could I not listen?" Ernesto de la Cruz embraced Miguel and then swept him up onto his shoulders, showing him off to the room. "I have a great-great-grandson!"

The crowd roared with applause.

Meanwhile, at the bottom of the hill, the silhouette of Frida Kahlo stepped up to the security guard.

"Honey, look! It's Frida!" someone yelled.

"Yes, it is I. Frida Kahlo," said the figure. The security guard immediately stood back and gestured her onto the cable car.

"It is an honor, señora!" the security guard exclaimed as she stepped on. The doors closed behind her. The "artist" adjusted her wig.

"I know," said Hector, heading up to Ernesto's mansion.

——

Ever since a musician **walked away** from their family,
the Riveras have avoided music . . .

. . . but **music** brings young Miguel Rivera life.

Miguel loves his friend **Dante** . . .

. . . and his **family**.

He also loves his **abuelita**, who works hard
to keep their family together.

Unfortunately, she works hard to keep them
away from music, too.

Miguel **needs a guitar** to show his family his talent.
He finds one in the mausoleum of Ernesto de la Cruz.

The moment he lays his hands on the guitar, he
disappears from the Land of the Living!

In the graveyard, the living can't see Miguel—
but **the dead can**!

He makes his way out of the graveyard and across
the Marigold Bridge to the **Land of the Dead**.

There, Miguel meets even more **family members**.
Just like his living relatives, they avoid music.

He also meets his great-great-grandmother
Mamá Imelda, who reminds him of Abuelita.

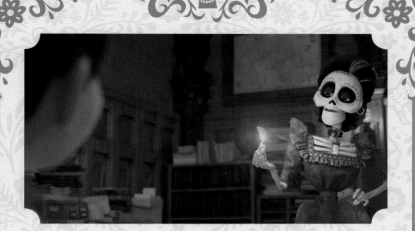

Mamá Imelda won't send Miguel home unless
he promises **not to play** music.

Mamá Imelda's **word is law** even in the afterlife.
No one will cross her.

Even though Miguel **loves his ancestors**,
he refuses to give up music . . .

. . . but if he doesn't get someone's blessing soon, he
might be **stuck forever** in the Land of the Dead.

Miguel, forgetting the time, chatted away with Ernesto and his guests. He relished the attention as the legendary singer barged into several party conversations, proudly introducing Miguel with giddy enthusiasm. The guests enjoyed watching Dante mingle, too.

In the main hall of the mansion, Miguel and Ernesto sat back on a lush sofa and enjoyed film clip after clip. Miguel couldn't tear his eyes away when one of his favorite films came on. In the film, the villainous character of Don Hidalgo raised two glasses to his peasant friend, played by Ernesto.

Miguel stood and acted out the scene as it played behind him. *"I would move heaven and earth for you, mi amigo. Salud!"* Miguel said, gesturing along with the villain. Ernesto looked on with delight. On the screen, Don Hidalgo and Ernesto's character each took a drink. Suddenly, the peasant spit out the drink.

"Poison!" Ernesto howled from the screen at the same time as Miguel. Miguel and his great-great-grandfather watched the ensuing fistfight between the two characters.

"You know, I did all my own stunts," Ernesto told Miguel. Miguel's eyes widened with amazement.

Later, Ernesto showed Miguel his ofrenda room,

which was filled with gifts from the living.

"All of this came from my amazing fans in the Land of the Living! They leave me more offerings than I know what to do with!" said Ernesto.

Miguel gazed around the room. Piled high were colorful breads, bottles of tequila, flowers, instruments, and sombreros.

Miguel thought about his family's ofrenda and the picture of Mamá Coco when she was a baby. She grew up only knowing her father by a torn picture on the altar. He wondered if this would happen to him, too, if he chose music over his family's plans. Would his photo be ripped, too? Would it be worth it? Ernesto knelt and looked into Miguel's eyes.

"Hey, what's wrong? Is it too much? You look overwhelmed."

"No, it's all great," said Miguel.

"But?" Ernesto asked.

Miguel gazed again at the massive piles of offerings.

"It's just, I've been looking up to you my whole life. You're the guy who actually did it! But . . ." Miguel paused. "Did you ever regret it? Choosing music over everything else?"

Ernesto sighed. "It was hard. Saying goodbye to Santa Cecilia. Heading off on my own . . ."

"Leaving your family?"

"Sí. But I could not have done it differently," Ernesto said. "One cannot deny who one is meant to be. And you, my great-great-grandson, are meant to be a musician!"

For the first time in his life, Miguel felt that someone understood his dream.

"You and I, we are artists, Miguel!" said Ernesto. "We cannot belong to one family. The world is our family!" He gestured dramatically to the sparkling city beyond his hilltop hacienda. Suddenly, fireworks boomed and lit up the night sky.

Chapter 19

As the guests moved outside to watch the fireworks, the main hall emptied and the lights dimmed. Ernesto and Miguel descended the staircase into the empty hall.

"Soon the party will move across town for my Sunrise Spectacular," Ernesto said. "Miguel, you must come to the show! You will be my guest of honor!"

Miguel's eyes lit up. "You mean it?"

"Of course, my boy!"

Miguel's chest filled with joy, then deflated. He lifted his shirt, revealing his now-skeletal ribs to Ernesto. "I can't. I have to go home before sunrise," he said sadly.

"I really do need to get you home," Ernesto said. He plucked a marigold petal from a vase and held it in front of Miguel. "It has been an honor. I am sorry to see you go, Miguel. I hope you die very soon—" He caught himself. "You know what I mean. Miguel, I give you my bles—"

"We had a deal, chamaco!" shouted a voice from the shadows. Miguel and Ernesto looked into the darkness but saw no one.

"Who are you? What is the meaning of this?" Ernesto asked. From out of the dark, Hector approached, still dressed as Frida Kahlo.

"Oh, Frida!" Ernesto said. "I thought you couldn't make it."

Hector yanked off his wig and colorful frock. "You said you'd take back my photo. You promised, Miguel." Hector stepped closer to them. Miguel backed into Ernesto's arms.

Ernesto rose to his feet and placed his hands protectively on Miguel's shoulders. He leaned down to whisper, "You know this, uh, man?"

"I just met him tonight. He told me he knew you."

Hector stepped forward with the photo, and Ernesto immediately recognized him. "H-Hector?" he stammered.

Hector ignored him. "Please, Miguel. Put my photo up."

He pushed the photo into Miguel's hands, but Ernesto intercepted it. He looked from the picture to the faded gray skeleton that stood before him. Hector looked away, as if embarrassed by his appearance. Ernesto stood there, stunned.

"My friend, you're—you're being forgotten," Ernesto said.

"And whose fault is that?" Hector snapped.

"Hector, please," said Ernesto.

"Those were my songs that you took. MY SONGS that made YOU famous."

"Wh-what?" Miguel asked.

"If I'm forgotten, it's because YOU never told anyone that I wrote them!"

"That's crazy!" Miguel interjected. "Ernesto wrote all his own songs."

Hector looked hard at the singer. "You wanna tell him, or should I?"

"Hector, I never meant to take credit," Ernesto said. "We made a great team, but you died, and I only sang your songs because I wanted to keep a part of you alive."

"Oh, how generous," Hector said sarcastically.

"You really did play together?" Miguel said.

"Look, I don't want to fight about it. I just want

you to make it right. Miguel can put my photo up—"

"Hector," Ernesto said softly.

"—and I can cross over the bridge. I can see my girl," Hector said.

Ernesto gazed at the photo, deliberating.

"Remember what you told me the night I left?" said Hector.

"That was a long time ago," said Ernesto.

"We drank together, and you told me you would move heaven and earth for your amigo. Well, I'm asking you to do that now."

"Heaven and earth?" Miguel asked. "Like in the movie?"

"What?" Hector said.

"That's Don Hidalgo's toast. In the movie *El Camino a Casa*."

"I'm talking about my REAL life, Miguel," Hector said.

"No, it's in there. Look," Miguel said, pointing to the movie clip being shown across the room.

Don Hidalgo was in the middle of his speech to the peasant Ernesto: *"Never were truer words spoken. This calls for a toast! To our friendship! I would move heaven and earth for you, mi amigo."*

"But in the movie," said Miguel, "Don Hidalgo

poisons the drink." He was starting to put the clues together.

"*Salud!*" shouted Don Hidalgo from the film. The two men drank.

Then Ernesto's character spit his out. "*Poison!*" he shouted, and the men tussled.

Hector looked from the film to Ernesto standing in front of him. His mind raced. "That night, Ernesto. The night I left . . ."

He remembered it well. They had been on tour, but he had missed his family too much, so he had packed up his songbook and grabbed his guitar case.

"*You wanna give up now?*" Ernesto asked. "*When we're this close to reaching our dream?*"

"*This was* your *dream,*" young Hector said. "*You'll manage.*"

"*I can't do this without your songs, Hector,*" Ernesto said, reaching for Hector's suitcase.

"*I'm going home, Ernesto,*" Hector said. "*Hate me if you want, but my mind is made up.*"

Ernesto had grown impatient, but he composed himself and switched on a charming smile. "*Oh, I could never hate you,*" he said. "*If you must go, then I'm . . . I'm sending you off with a toast!*" The singer poured a couple of drinks and handed one to Hector.

"To our friendship. I would move heaven and earth for you, mi amigo. Salud!" They both drank.

Ernesto had walked Hector to the train station, but when Hector stumbled, Ernesto simply took his suitcase. Hector had thought the pain in his stomach was from something he had eaten.

"Perhaps it was that chorizo, my friend," young Ernesto said.

"Or something I drank," Hector said, snapping back to the present. "I woke up dead." He directed a steely gaze at Ernesto. "You . . . poisoned me."

"You're confusing movies with reality, Hector," Ernesto assured him.

Suddenly, visions of Ernesto's betrayal flashed before Hector like old film clips on a continuous loop. Hector remembered that as he had lain collapsed on the cold street, his suitcase had been opened. A hand had reached in and stolen his songbook.

"All this time, I thought it was just bad luck," Hector said. "I never thought that you might have . . . that you . . ." He clenched his jaw, then lunged at Ernesto, tackling him to the ground.

"Hector!" Miguel shouted.

"How could you!" Hector yelled at Ernesto.

"Security! Security!" cried Ernesto.

Miguel looked on in shock as the two men scuffled on the floor. He struggled to understand everything Hector had said about the toast, the songbook, and waking up dead. Could it be true? Could Ernesto have poisoned Hector?

"You took everything away from me!" Hector shouted as security guards rushed in. He resisted as they pulled him off Ernesto, but it was no use. "You rat!"

"Have him taken care of. He's not well," Ernesto ordered.

"I just wanted to go back home!" Hector cried. Miguel felt a lump in his throat as the guards dragged Hector out of the room. "No, no, NO!"

Miguel was left alone with Ernesto. His mind raced as he tried to figure out what to do next.

"I apologize. Where were we?"

"You were going to give me your blessing," Miguel said, unsure after everything he'd just heard. Was his great-great-grandfather responsible for Hector's death?

"Yes. Uh, sí," Ernesto said. He plucked a marigold petal, but hesitated. "Miguel, my reputation, it is very important to me. I would hate to have you think—"

"That you murdered Hector for his songs?" asked Miguel, a knot growing in his stomach.

"You don't think that. Do you?"

"I . . . No. Everyone knows you're the . . . the good guy," Miguel said, but doubt had set in, and it oozed in his voice.

Ernesto abruptly shoved the photo of Hector into his suit pocket.

"Papá Ernesto? My blessing?" Miguel asked.

Ernesto crumpled the marigold petal. "Security!" he shouted. His guards appeared at the doorway. "Take care of Miguel. He'll be extending his stay." The guards grabbed Miguel by the shoulder.

Miguel's face burned with anger. "What! But I'm your family!" he yelled. He couldn't believe what was happening.

"And Hector was my best friend," Ernesto said coldly.

Miguel went pale. "You *did* murder him."

"Success doesn't come for free, Miguel. You have to be willing to do whatever it takes—to seize your moment. I know you understand."

Chapter 20

"Let go!" Miguel protested as the guards dragged him out the back of Ernesto's mansion. They threw him into a large cenote, or sinkhole.

"No!" Miguel hollered as he fell, finally crashing into water at the bottom of the cenote. He struggled against the deep, dark water, fighting his way back to the surface. Splashing about, he spotted a stone island. "Help!" He paddled over to it. "Can anyone hear me? I wanna go home!" He reached the stone island and collapsed against it.

Miguel's soaked hoodie sagged off him, revealing that his skeletal transition was almost complete. He gazed up to the sky. He had to get out. He had to get home, but how? He was alone. He dropped his head, hopeless. Suddenly, he heard footsteps. Hector emerged from the darkness and stumbled toward Miguel, who lay at the water's edge.

"Hector?" Miguel cried.

"Kid?" Hector shouted.

"Oh, Hector!" They ran to each other. Hector embraced Miguel. Overcome with shame, Miguel lowered his head. "You were right. I should have gone back to my family—" he said.

"Hey, hey, hey," Hector said as he patted him gently.

"They told me not to be like Ernesto, but I didn't listen."

"It's okay," Hector said.

"I told them I didn't care if they remembered me. I didn't care if I was on their stupid ofrenda." Miguel sobbed against Hector's chest. Hector held him close.

"Hey, chamaco, it's okay. It's okay."

Miguel took a deep breath. "I told them I didn't care."

Suddenly, a gold flicker fluttered through Hector's bones. "Huuuh!" he exclaimed, and fell to his knees.

"Hector!" Miguel screamed, scared at what was happening to his friend.

"She's . . . forgetting me," Hector said. Miguel watched him with despair.

"Who?"

"My daughter."

"She's the reason you wanted to cross the bridge?"

"I just wanted to see her again," Hector said softly. "I never should have left Santa Cecilia. Ernesto convinced me that my 'big moment' was waiting for me far away from home, but . . ." He gulped for breath. "I wish I could apologize. I wish I could tell her that her papá was trying to come home. That he loved her so much." Hector looked toward the sky. "My Coco . . ."

A chill ran through Miguel.

"Coco?" Miguel reached into his hoodie and looked at the photo of Mamá Imelda, baby Coco, and the faceless musician. Miguel showed it to Hector.

Hector's eyes narrowed as he stared at familiar faces from long ago. "Where—where did you get this?" he asked.

"That's my Mamá Coco. That's my Mamá Imelda. Is that—" Miguel pointed at the headless musician. "You?"

"We're . . . family?" Hector said finally, smiling at his great-great-grandson. Miguel grinned back at his Papá Hector. Family. It felt right.

Hector returned his gaze to the photo and his

smile faded. He touched the image of baby Coco. "I always hoped I'd see her again. That she'd miss me. Maybe put up my photo. But it never happened," Hector said. His voice lowered to a whisper. "You know the worst part?"

Miguel shook his head.

"Even if I never got to see Coco in the living world, I thought at least one day I'd see her here. Give her the biggest hug. But she's the last person who remembers me. The moment she's gone from the living world . . ."

"You disappear from this one. You'll never get to see her."

"Ever again," Hector finished. He sat there quiet for a moment. "You know, I wrote her a song once. We used to sing it every night, at the same time. No matter how far apart we were. What I wouldn't give to sing it to her one last time." Hector sang his original version of "Remember Me" in a soft voice. It was a much different version from Ernesto's. Miguel thought it was beautiful.

When the last note faded, Miguel said, "He stole your guitar. He stole your songs. YOU should be the one the world remembers, not him!"

"I didn't write 'Remember Me' for the world. I

wrote it for Coco," he said. "I'm a pretty sorry excuse for a great-great-grandpa."

"Are you kidding? A minute ago, I thought I was related to a murderer. You're a total upgrade."

Hector couldn't muster a smile.

"My whole life, there's been something that made me different . . . and I never knew where it came from," Miguel said. "But now I know. It came from YOU!" He gave Hector a wide smile. "I'm proud we're family!" Miguel looked up to the top of the hole, where he was tossed down. "I'm proud to be his family! TRRRRRRRRAI-HAY-HAY-HAY-HAAAY!" he yelled in a grito.

Hector perked up and followed Miguel's grito. "TRRRRRRRRAAAAI-HAAAAY-HAAAAAY! I'm proud to be HIS family!" They exchanged gritos until the cenote echoed with the sound. Soon, though, the echo faded. They were still stuck.

Then something echoed back to them.

"Rooo-roooo-rooooooo!"

Miguel and Hector looked up, amazed.

"Dante?" Miguel said.

"Rooooooooooo-roo-roo-rooo!" Dante howled and poked his head through the opening above them.

"Dante!" Miguel shouted and laughed. "It's Dante!"

Dante panted and wagged his tail happily. Behind him were two more figures peeking down at them. It was Mamá Imelda and Pepita. Pepita released a roar that shook the whole cavern. Miguel and Mamá Imelda laughed with joy.

"Imelda!" Hector yelled up at her with a charming smile.

Mamá Imelda's relief turned to coldness. "Hector."

"You look good. . . ." Hector offered a smile.

Chapter
21

Pepita flew out of the cenote and ascended toward the clouds, carrying Imelda, Hector, Miguel, and Dante on her back. Miguel hugged Dante fiercely.

"Dante, you KNEW he was my Papá Hector the whole time! You were trying to bring us together! You *are* a real spirit guide!" Miguel praised him. "Who's a good spirit guide? *You* are!" Dante smiled dumbly at Miguel. Suddenly, before Miguel's eyes, neon patterns spread outward from Dante's paws. "Whoa!" Miguel gasped as little wings sprouted on Dante's back.

Dante spread his new wings and jumped up to fly. But he plummeted beneath the clouds!

"Dante!" Miguel shouted, and then Dante was

back up, flapping goofily and barking his head off. He was a full-blown spirit guide.

Pepita flew into the small plaza where the other dead members of the Rivera family waited.

"Look, there they are!" Papá Julio exclaimed, pointing as they landed. The entire family rushed over to Miguel, rambling excitedly.

"He's all right! Oh, thank goodness!"

Hector dismounted from Pepita's back first and raised a hand to help Imelda down. She glared at him, dismissing his help.

Miguel stroked Dante lovingly. Pepita gave Miguel a big lick.

Mamá Imelda pulled Miguel into a tight hug. "M'ijo, I was so worried! Thank goodness we found you in time!" Her eyes fell on Hector, who held his hat in his hands sheepishly. "And YOU! How many times must I turn you away?"

"Imelda," Hector said softly.

"I want nothing to do with you. Not in life, not in death." She glared at him. "I spent decades protecting my family from your mistakes. He spends five minutes with you and I have to fish him out of a sinkhole!"

Miguel stepped between Mamá Imelda and Hector. "I wasn't in there because of Hector. He was in there because of me," he explained. "He was just trying to get me home. I didn't want to listen, but he was right. Nothing is more important than family."

Mamá Imelda raised her eyebrows at Hector.

"I'm ready to accept your blessing. And your conditions. But first I need to find Ernesto. To get Hector's photo," said Miguel.

"What?" Mamá Imelda said.

"So he can see Coco again. Hector should be on our ofrenda. He's part of our family."

"He left this family!" Mamá Imelda exclaimed.

"He tried to go home to you and Coco, but Ernesto murdered him!"

She looked to Hector for confirmation.

"It's true, Imelda," Hector said.

Many emotions flickered across Imelda's face. "And so what if it's true? You leave me alone with a child to raise and I'm just supposed to forgive you?"

"Imelda, I—"

Hector's body shimmered, leaving him winded. Imelda gasped.

"I'm running out of time, Imelda," Hector pleaded. "It's Coco."

Mamá Imelda stared at him, trying to understand what was happening. "She's forgetting you."

"You don't have to forgive him, but we shouldn't forget him," Miguel said.

"Oh, Hector, I wanted to forget you. I wanted Coco to forget you too, but . . ."

"This is my fault, not yours," Hector said. "I'm sorry, Imelda."

Mamá Imelda, holding in her emotions, turned to Miguel. "Miguel, if we help you get his photo, you will return home? No more music?"

"Family comes first," Miguel said.

Mamá Imelda considered the situation. She turned to Hector. "I—I can't forgive you, but I will help you."

Miguel smiled.

"So how do we get to Ernesto?" Mamá Imelda asked.

"I might know a way," Miguel answered.

Chapter 22

Hundreds were gathered to watch Ernesto's Sunrise Spectacular. On the huge, freestanding stage, Frida's dramatic performance piece swelled with symphonic music as a giant papaya ignited. The papaya seeds unfurled to reveal dancers dressed like Frida Kahlo, with thickly painted unibrows. The Frida clones gyrated their bodies nonsensically as they rolled out of the flaming papaya. Next, a giant cactus that resembled Frida was illuminated. All the dancers slunk into it. In the midst of all this, nine Riveras, dressed as cloned Frida dancers, inched their way out of the spotlight and toward the wings.

"Good luck, muchacho!" the real Frida Kahlo said to Miguel.

"Gracias, Frida!" Miguel waved, running backstage

with the rest of his family. Once there, they swiftly shed their Frida costumes, and Dante popped out from under Tío Óscar's skirt. Mamá Imelda was tangled up in her frock.

"Here, let me help you with—" Hector said.

"Don't touch me," she snapped.

The family joined together in a huddle. "Everyone clear on the plan?" Miguel asked.

"Find Hector's photo," Tía Victoria said.

"Give it to Miguel," Papá Julio added.

"Send Miguel home," Mamá Imelda said.

"Got your petals?" asked Hector.

Each family member raised a marigold petal. Imelda led the way out of the backstage corridor. "Now we just have to find Ernesto . . . ," she said, turning a corner and suddenly finding herself face to face with the famous crooner.

Ernesto turned to Mamá Imelda, smiling. "Yes?" he said.

"Ah!" she exclaimed. The family stopped in their tracks, still hidden from Ernesto's view.

His smile dropped. "Don't I know you?"

Imelda slipped off her shoes in one swift motion and smacked Ernesto across the face with it. "That's for murdering the love of my life!"

Ernesto looked confused. "Who the . . . ?"

Hector rounded the corner.

"She's talking about me!" He turned to Mamá Imelda. "I'm the love of your life?"

"I don't know! I'm still angry at you."

Ernesto gasped. "Hector? How did you—"

Imelda smacked him again. "And that's for trying to murder my grandson!"

"Grandson?" Ernesto muttered, confused. Now Miguel jumped out of the corridor, and Ernesto pieced it together. "You! Wait—you're related to Hector?"

Miguel spied Hector's photo in Ernesto's pocket.

"The photo!" Miguel cried. The rest of the Riveras closed in on the singer. Ernesto turned to run.

"After him!" Mamá Imelda yelled. Ernesto disappeared below the stage, where his rising platform was set up for his big entrance.

He cried out for help. "Security! Ayúdame!"

The Rivera family fanned out after him. Hector ran next to Imelda. "You said love of your life!"

"I don't know what I said!"

"That's what I heard," Miguel chimed in.

"Can we focus on the matter at hand?" Mamá Imelda pleaded. The security guards had arrived, and the family fought. Papá Julio kicked a guard.

Tío Felipe pulled Tío Óscar's arms off and spun them around, knocking down the guards like dominoes. Tío Óscar pounced on the remaining guard. Ernesto escaped through the stage door. Suddenly, a stagehand was in front of him.

"You're on in thirty seconds, señor," said the stagehand. Ernesto shoved him out of the way, sending him flying. While more security guards showed up to wrangle the Riveras, Mamá Imelda reached Ernesto and lunged for Hector's photo. Miguel tackled him, and the photo fell. Mamá Imelda grabbed it.

"Miguel, I have it!" she called, tumbling backward. Miguel tried to turn to help her, but guards chased him away. Suddenly, Mamá Imelda rose into the air. She was on Ernesto's rising platform!

As she ascended to the stage, Ernesto raced up the stairs.

Miguel's family blocked the guards from chasing Mamá Imelda. She was all alone.

Chapter 23

"Ladies and gentlemen, the one, the only—Ernesto de la Cruz!" shouted the announcer. The audience exploded with wild applause. The platform stopped at the top, and the spotlight shone on Mamá Imelda. Neon letters spelling ERNESTO! blasted brightly behind her.

Meanwhile, Ernesto himself had arrived at the stage's right wing. He pointed at Mamá Imelda. "Get her off the stage!" he ordered his security guards, and they hustled up there, scaling the set to get to her.

To the left of the stage, directly opposite where Ernesto stood, Miguel and his family spotted Mamá Imelda above them. The spotlight illuminated her. They watched, helpless, as she stood frozen above the audience while the guards closed in on her.

Miguel's mind raced. He glanced at the audience. They were growing restless. "Sing!" he suddenly yelled to his great-great-grandmother.

If she could muster a song, maybe the audience would cheer and the guards would have to back off. Hopefully, that would give them enough time to secure the photograph.

"Sing!" he cried again.

Seeing the guards approaching, Mamá Imelda nodded at Miguel. She grabbed the microphone, closed her eyes, and started to sing.

Miguel gave Hector a guitar and placed a mic stand in front of him. Tía Rosita connected a pair of cords while Tía Victoria flipped a knob on a soundboard. Hector strummed the guitar, which was amplified through the speakers.

On the stage, the guards stopped at the edge of her spotlight. Mamá Imelda sang as she descended the staircase. The spotlight followed her every move. As she came down, she made eye contact with Hector. He gave her a sweet smile. Imelda's eyes glinted with tears at the memories of them singing together long ago. Then she straightened and belted out a lively ballad.

The audience was on their feet, clapping along.

Ernesto grunted. Soon the stage conductor joined in with the whole orchestra. Mamá Imelda twirled across the stage, moving away from the security guards and closer to her family. One guard tried to block her, but she grabbed him to dance. Afraid of the spotlight, he ran off. She had almost joined her family when suddenly someone's hand was on her wrist. A voice joined her in harmony. The spotlight widened to reveal Ernesto de la Cruz singing, too. The crowd went wild. As they sang, he danced Mamá Imelda around the stage, trying to get Hector's photo back.

"Let go of me!" Mamá Imelda threatened between verses. At the song's finale, Imelda stomped her heel on Ernesto's foot on his high note, and he released her.

"Ay, ay, ay, ay!" he cried. The crowd cheered at his wild grito while Mamá Imelda fled with the photo. She rushed to embrace Hector backstage.

"I forgot what that felt like." Mamá Imelda blushed and pulled away from him awkwardly.

"You still got it," Hector said. The two smiled at each other, softening.

"Ahem!" Miguel cleared his throat to get their attention.

"Oh!" Mamá Imelda said. She handed the photo of Hector to Miguel and pulled out her petal.

"Miguel, I give you my blessing," she said as the petal began to glow. "To go home. To put up our photos. And to never . . ."

Miguel looked slightly saddened, anticipating the condition.

"Never play music again," he offered with lowered eyes.

Mamá Imelda smiled. "To never forget how much your family loves you."

The petal surged higher. Miguel brightened, touched by her words.

"You're going home," Hector said.

"You're not going anywhere!" snarled Ernesto de la Cruz.

Chapter
24

Ernesto yanked Miguel away by his hood before the petal could swoosh him home. Mamá Imelda lunged at him, but he shoved her to the floor. Papá Julio and the uncles arrived, but it was too late. Behind the set was the open air and a view of the city—and a thousand-foot drop to the water. Ernesto heaved Miguel onto the ledge over the water. Miguel looked down.

"Stay back! Stay back. All of you!" Ernesto threatened. The family closed in anyway. "Stay back! Not one more step."

Though weak, Hector pleaded, "Ernesto, stop! Leave the boy alone!" He stumbled, shimmering like before, then collapsed to the floor.

Ernesto shook his head, clutching Miguel atop the

ledge. "I've worked too hard, Hector. Too hard to let him destroy everything."

Behind Ernesto, Tía Rosita commandeered one of the cameras and pointed it toward the action. In the makeshift sound booth, Tía Victoria pushed a volume dial up. Soon the image of Ernesto holding Miguel hostage was projected onto the massive stadium screens. The audience hushed as they watched the drama unfold.

"He's a living child, Ernesto!" Hector called out, trying to reason with him. Miguel tried to escape from the singer.

"He's a threat!" Ernesto said, still holding Miguel by his hood. "You think I'd let him go back to the Land of the Living with your photo? To keep your memory alive? No."

"You're a coward!" Miguel yelled, wriggling to get free from his grasp.

"I am Ernesto de la Cruz. The greatest musician of all time!"

"Hector's the REAL musician. You're just the guy who murdered him and stole his songs!"

The crowd gasped.

"Murder?" someone cried.

"I am the one who is willing to do what it takes to seize my moment—whatever it takes!" Ernesto roared. He swung Miguel out over the ledge. Miguel screamed, grasping for Ernesto. Ernesto released his grip, and Miguel began to fall.

"No!" Mamá Imelda cried, running to the ledge.

The audience shrieked as the fight played out on the monitors.

Ernesto, unaware that the audience had witnessed his treachery, coolly moved away. He passed Hector, who remained on the floor. "Apologies, old friend, but the show must go on."

The Rivera family rushed to the ledge. As he fell, Miguel heard a faint howling. Like a lightning bolt, Dante sliced through the air. He caught Miguel's shirt in his teeth and extended his wings. He and Miguel jolted with the movement, and Hector's photo slipped from Miguel's hands.

"Ahh—no!" Miguel wailed as the photo drifted out of sight. Miguel and Dante twisted in the air as Dante desperately tried to reverse their descent, but they were too heavy. Though Dante struggled to keep a grip on Miguel's shirt, it ripped from his sharp teeth, and Miguel again fell toward the water. He thought he was done for, but at the last second, Pepita scooped him up in her talons. Safe, Miguel looked down at the water. Hector's photo was gone.

Chapter
25

Ernesto stepped up to the stage curtain. He slicked his hair back and emerged to face his audience. The spotlight zoomed in on him.

"Ha, ha!" Ernesto said in greeting. The audience responded with loud boos. He stepped back.

"Boo! Murderer!" the crowd shouted.

"Please, please, mi familia," said Ernesto, trying to calm them, but the heckling and boos grew louder.

"Get off the stage!"

"Orchestra! The music. A-one, a-two, a-one—" Ernesto gestured.

The conductor glared at Ernesto and broke his baton. Through the booing, Ernesto tried to sing "Remember Me," but the crowd pelted him with fruit.

"Look!" hollered someone in the audience, and

they all pointed up to the screens. Pepita rose above the ledge with Miguel on her back. Miguel slid down her wing and ran to his family.

"He's all right!" the crowd cheered.

Ernesto looked from one of the screens to the audience, back and forth, until he saw Pepita growing larger as she prowled past the camera. Ernesto slowly backed away just as Pepita lurched through the curtain, her glowing eyes locked on him.

"Nice kitty!" Ernesto whimpered. Pepita flung him into the air like a ball of yarn. "Aaahhh! Put me down! No, please! I beg you, stop! Stop! NO!" Pepita continued to swing him around, gaining momentum, until she finally released him over the audience. "No!" he screeched, soaring over them and out of the stadium. A few moments later, he hit a giant church bell in the distance, and everyone heard the loud clang.

Back in the stadium, the audience erupted into cheers. Mamá Imelda ran to Miguel and embraced him. "Miguel!" she said. Hector struggled to his feet.

Miguel rushed to support him. "Hector! The photo, I lost it . . . ," he sobbed.

"It's okay, m'ijo. It's—" Suddenly, his body flickered

violently. He moaned and collapsed. Miguel knelt next to him.

"Hector! Hector?"

Hector looked up weakly. "My Coco . . ."

"No! We can still find the photo!" Miguel cried.

Mamá Imelda looked to the horizon, where the first rays of sunlight peeked over. "Miguel, it's almost sunrise!"

"No, no, no—I can't leave you."

Hector gazed at Miguel. The skeletal transformation was creeping along the edges of Miguel's face. He was almost a full skeleton now. "We're both out of time, m'ijo." Hector's bones continued to shimmer.

"No, no, she can't forget you!" Miguel said.

"I just wanted her to know that I loved her." Hector grabbed a marigold petal.

"Hector . . . ," Miguel said.

"You have our blessing, Miguel," said Hector.

"No conditions," added Mamá Imelda.

The petal glowed. Hector struggled to lift the petal to Miguel. Mamá Imelda tenderly took his hand in hers to help.

"No, Papá Hector, please!"

Imelda and Hector moved their joined hands

toward Miguel's chest. Hector's eyelids began to close. "Go home," he whispered.

"I promise I won't let Coco forget you!" Miguel yelled as a swirl of marigolds covered him.

Whoosh! He was gone.

Chapter
26

Miguel was back in Ernesto's mausoleum. Dazed, he looked through the window. The day had broken. On the floor was the skull guitar. Miguel snatched it up, exited the mausoleum, and ran out of the cemetery. He raced through the plaza, past the statue of Ernesto de la Cruz, and toward home. He blew right past his Tío Berto and Primo Abel.

"There he is!" Tío Berto said. Surprised, Primo Abel fell off the bench. Just then, Papá came around the corner, but Miguel ran past him.

"Miguel? Stop!"

Miguel raced on, following the trail of marigolds through the front gate. He darted for the back bedroom to find Mamá Coco. Just as he made it to the doorway, Abuelita stepped into his path.

"Where have you been?" she asked.

"Ah! I need to see Mamá Coco, please!"

She noticed Miguel gripping a guitar in his hand. "What are you doing with that! Give it to me!"

Miguel rushed past Abuelita and slammed the door shut behind him.

"Miguel! Stop! Miguel!"

Miguel locked the door. Mamá Coco stared into space, her eyes completely vacant.

Miguel looked into her eyes. "Mamá Coco? Can you hear me? It's Miguel. I saw your papá. Remember? Papá? Please—if you forget him, he'll be gone forever!"

She sat and stared in silence while Miguel's father banged on the door.

"Miguel, open this door!"

Miguel continued. He had to get through to Mamá Coco. He showed her the guitar. "Here, this was his guitar, right? He used to play it for you? See, there he is." Mamá Coco stared as if Miguel weren't even there. "Papá, remember? Papá?"

"Miguel!" Papá yelled at him through the door.

"Mamá Coco, please, don't forget him," Miguel pleaded.

Soon a bunch of keys rattled. The door was flung open and the family poured in.

"What are you doing to that poor woman?" Abuelita cried, and pushed Miguel aside. "It's okay, Mamita, it's okay."

"What's gotten into you?" Papá said to Miguel.

Miguel looked down, defeated. Tears dripped off his nose. Papá's anger gave way to relief. He embraced his son. "I thought I'd lost you, Miguel. . . ."

"I'm sorry, Papá."

Miguel's mamá stepped forward. "We're all together now. That's what matters," she said.

"Not all of us," Miguel mumbled, thinking of Hector.

"It's okay, Mamita. Miguel, you apologize to your Mamá Coco!" Abuelita demanded. Miguel approached Mamá Coco.

"Mamá Coco . . . ," Miguel began. He glanced at Hector's guitar.

"Well? Apologize!"

Suddenly, Miguel knew what he had to do. "Mamá Coco? Your papá—he wanted you to have this." He picked up the guitar.

Abuelita started to intervene, but Miguel's father stopped her with a tender pat on her arm. "Mamá, wait," he said, watching his son.

Miguel started to sing "Remember Me" the way

131

Hector had sung it. He poured himself into the song.

"Look," Miguel's mother said as the glimmer in the old woman's eyes grew brighter with every note. Her cheeks plumped. Her lips arched into a smile. Miguel noticed the change, too.

Abuelita stood watching, bewildered.

Soon Mamá Coco joined Miguel in singing the song she used to sing with her father. Tears streamed down Abuelita's cheeks. Mamá Coco looked over at her daughter, concerned.

"Elena? What's wrong, m'ija?"

"Nothing, Mamá. Nothing at all."

Mamá Coco turned to Miguel. "My papá used to sing me that song."

"He loved you, Mamá Coco. Your papá loved you so much," Miguel said.

A smile spread across Mamá Coco's face. She'd waited a long time to hear those words. She turned to her nightstand and opened a drawer. She pulled out a notebook and peeled back the lining to reveal a torn scrap of paper. She handed it to Miguel.

It was the missing face from the photo—Hector's face! Miguel pieced the picture back together. Mamá Coco smiled.

"Papá was a musician," she said. "When I was a little girl, he and Mamá would sing such beautiful songs. . . ."

The family gathered around Mamá Coco. It was time to learn about Papá Hector.

Chapter 27

A year later, the cemetery was once again filled with families cleaning off headstones and laying flowers. At Ernesto de la Cruz's mausoleum, there weren't as many offerings or as many fans as the year before. Someone had spray-painted FORGET YOU on a sign that hung by the statue.

A tour group moved through the town and stopped in front of Rivera Family Shoemakers. "And right over here, one of Santa Cecilia's greatest treasures," said the guide. The group crowded in to listen. "The home of the esteemed songwriter Hector Rivera. The letters Hector wrote home for his daughter, Coco, contain the lyrics for all your favorite songs, not just

'Remember Me.'" The tourists snapped pictures of the skull guitar and framed letters.

In the courtyard, Miguel's cousins Rosa and Abel hung colorful papel picado while Miguel's parents worked on tamales. Miguel's grandfather swept the courtyard as the tiny grandchildren created a marigold-petal path leading to the ofrenda room.

"And that man is your Papá Julio," Miguel explained, holding his ten-month-old sister in his arms while Abuelita arranged photos on the altars. The baby had been named Socorro after Mamá Coco's full name. "And there is Tía Rosita, and your Tía Victoria, and those two are Óscar and Felipe. These aren't just old pictures—they're our family, and they're counting on us to remember them."

Abuelita smiled to see that her grandson was passing on the tradition of Día de los Muertos to his baby sister. She gently placed one last picture frame on the ofrenda. It was a photo of Mamá Coco. Abuelita exchanged a glance with Miguel, and he put an arm around her. They both missed Mamá Coco very much. Next to her picture was the photo of Mamá Imelda, Coco, and Hector, taped together again.

—

Back in the Land of the Dead, Hector waited in the departures line. After so many years of being rejected, he was full of nerves.

"Enjoy your visit! Next!" called the departures agent. Hector stepped up to the monitor. The agent recognized him and smirked. Hector chuckled nervously as the agent scanned him.

Ding!

"Enjoy your visit, Hector!" the agent exclaimed.

Hector's chest swelled with joy. His family had finally included his picture on the family ofrenda. Mamá Imelda joined him at the foot of the bridge. They kissed until a joyful voice cried out.

"Papá!"

Hector turned to see his daughter walking toward them. He opened his arms to give Coco a huge embrace. "Coco!" he exclaimed, holding her tight. He knew that every moment together was a miracle. Coco took a hand of each of her parents, and together they crossed the bridge.

Overhead, Dante and Pepita flew in the night sky of the Land of the Dead. They alighted on the marigold path and bounded across and into the Land of the Living. Dante's neon skin and wings disappeared, and he was a normal hairless Xolo once more. Pepita's shadow of a glorious winged feline loomed large, but as she rounded the corner into the Land of the Living, she appeared as a little alley cat. Dante and Pepita weaved past holiday revelers and into the Riveras' courtyard. Abuelita spotted Dante and quickly tossed him a tamale. He chomped it down.

In the courtyard, the family gathered around Miguel as he strummed his guitar and began to sing. Dante hopped up to give him a lick on the cheek.

"Dante!" Miguel squealed. Everyone laughed.

On this special night of Día de los Muertos, the spirits of Papá Hector and Mamá Imelda stood arm in arm, listening to Miguel play. Abuelita listened, too, with Mamá Coco's hand on her shoulder. Miguel's father cradled the baby as Miguel's mother leaned on him. All of Miguel's family, living and dead, bobbed their heads to the melody while others sang along and played their own instruments. Though the living couldn't see the dead, the family was whole, brought together by the harmony—and the meaning—of a song.